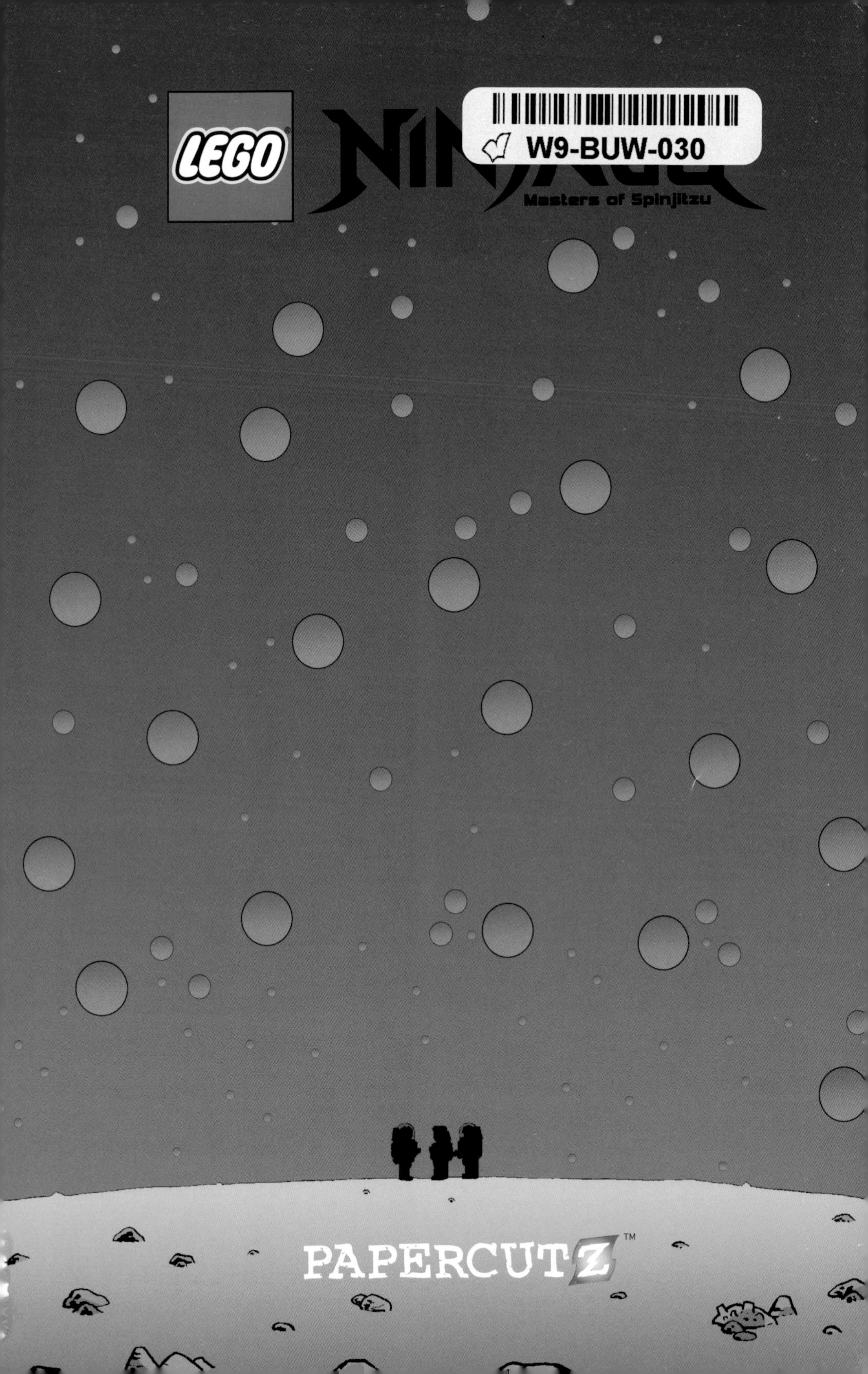
LEGO
NINJAGO
Masters of Spinjitzu
PAPERCUTZ

LEGO® GRAPHIC NOVELS AVAILABLE FROM PAPERCUTZ™

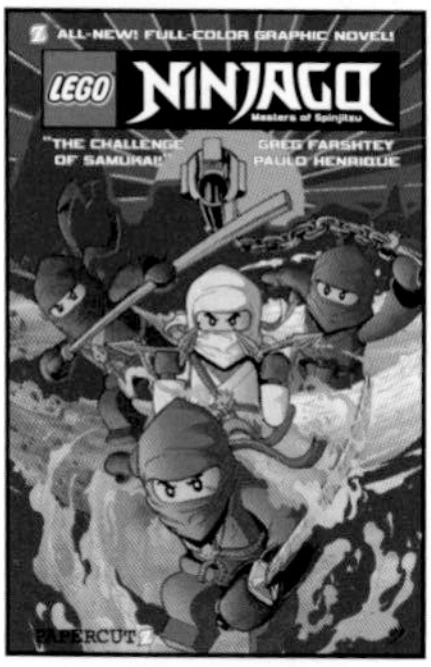
ALL-NEW! FULL-COLOR GRAPHIC NOVEL!
LEGO NINJAGO
"THE CHALLENGE OF SAMUKAI"
GREG FARSHTEY
PAULO HENRIQUE
PAPERCUTZ
LEGO NINJAGO #1

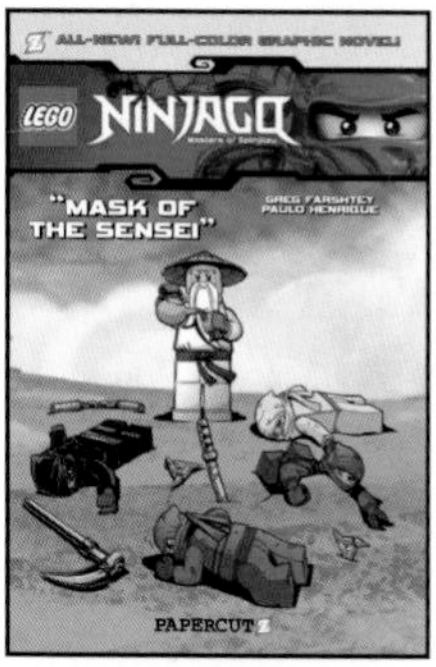
ALL-NEW! FULL-COLOR GRAPHIC NOVEL!
LEGO NINJAGO
"MASK OF THE SENSEI"
GREG FARSHTEY
PAULO HENRIQUE
PAPERCUTZ
LEGO NINJAGO #2

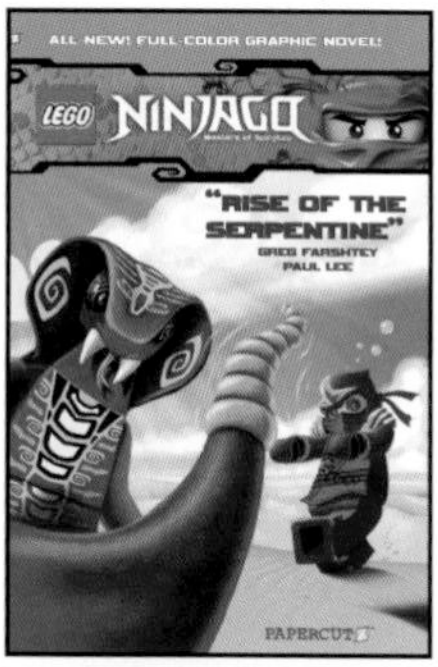
ALL-NEW! FULL-COLOR GRAPHIC NOVEL!
LEGO NINJAGO
"RISE OF THE SERPENTINE"
GREG FARSHTEY
PAUL LEE
PAPERCUTZ
LEGO NINJAGO #3

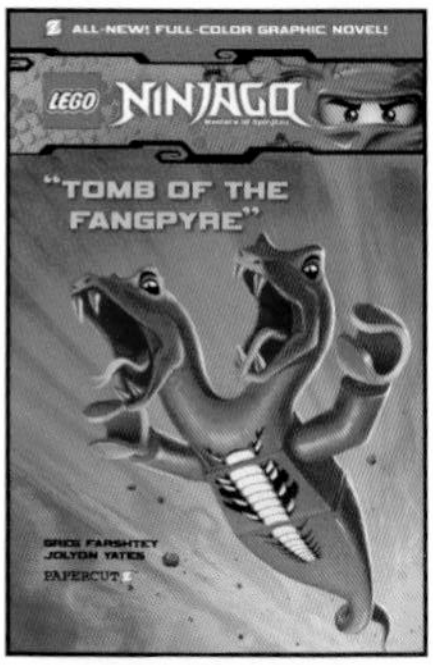
ALL-NEW! FULL-COLOR GRAPHIC NOVEL!
LEGO NINJAGO
"TOMB OF THE FANGPYRE"
GREG FARSHTEY
JOLYON YATES
PAPERCUTZ
LEGO NINJAGO #4

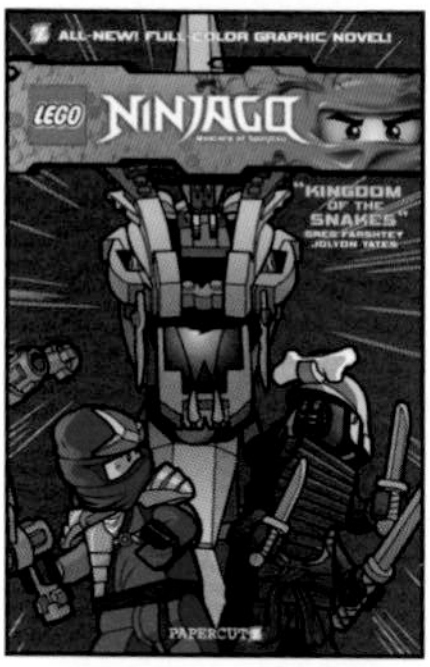
ALL-NEW! FULL-COLOR GRAPHIC NOVEL!
LEGO NINJAGO
"KINGDOM OF THE SNAKES"
GREG FARSHTEY
JOLYON YATES
PAPERCUTZ
LEGO NINJAGO #5

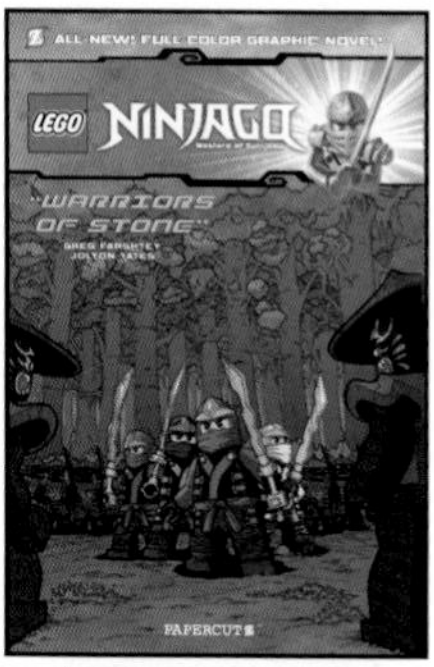
ALL-NEW! FULL-COLOR GRAPHIC NOVEL!
LEGO NINJAGO
"WARRIORS OF STONE"
GREG FARSHTEY
JOLYON YATES
PAPERCUTZ
LEGO NINJAGO #6

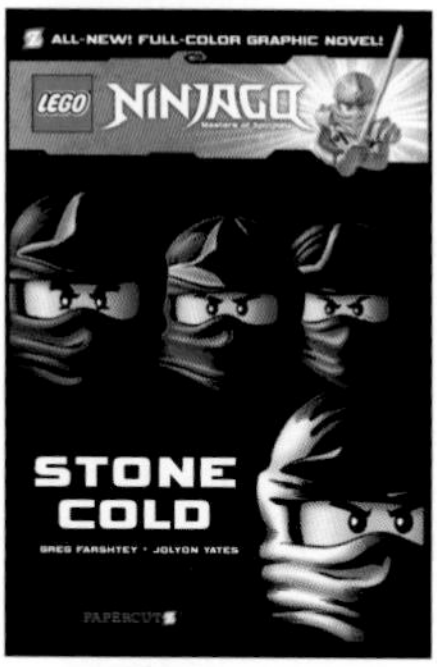
ALL-NEW! FULL-COLOR GRAPHIC NOVEL!
LEGO NINJAGO
STONE COLD
GREG FARSHTEY • JOLYON YATES
PAPERCUTZ
LEGO NINJAGO #7

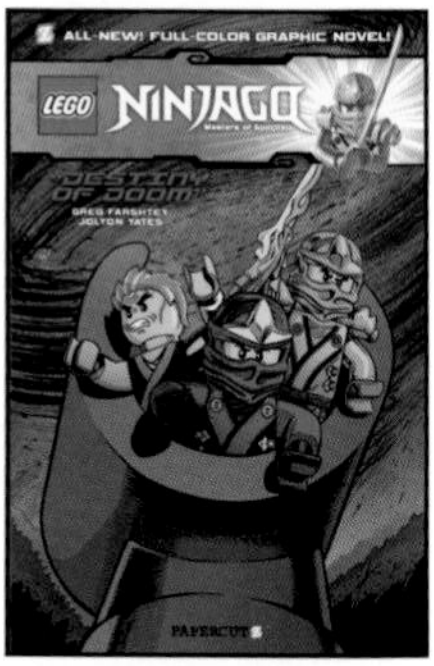
ALL-NEW! FULL-COLOR GRAPHIC NOVEL!
LEGO NINJAGO
"DESTINY OF DOOM"
GREG FARSHTEY
JOLYON YATES
PAPERCUTZ
LEGO NINJAGO #8

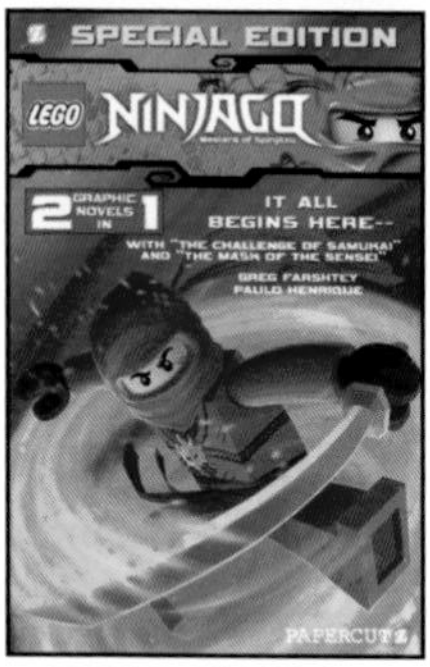
SPECIAL EDITION
LEGO NINJAGO
2 GRAPHIC NOVELS IN 1
IT ALL BEGINS HERE--
WITH "THE CHALLENGE OF SAMUKAI" AND "THE MASK OF THE SENSEI"
GREG FARSHTEY
PAULO HENRIQUE
PAPERCUTZ
SPECIAL EDITION #1
(Features stories from
NINJAGO #1 & #2.)

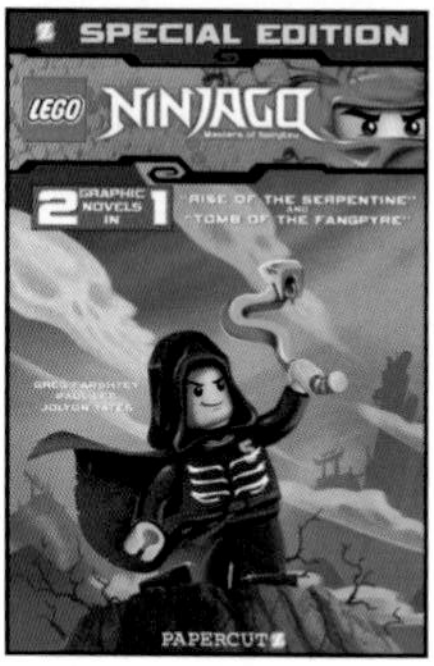
SPECIAL EDITION
LEGO NINJAGO
2 GRAPHIC NOVELS IN 1
"RISE OF THE SERPENTINE"
"TOMB OF THE FANGPYRE"
PAPERCUTZ
SPECIAL EDITION #2
(Features stories from
NINJAGO #3 & #4.)

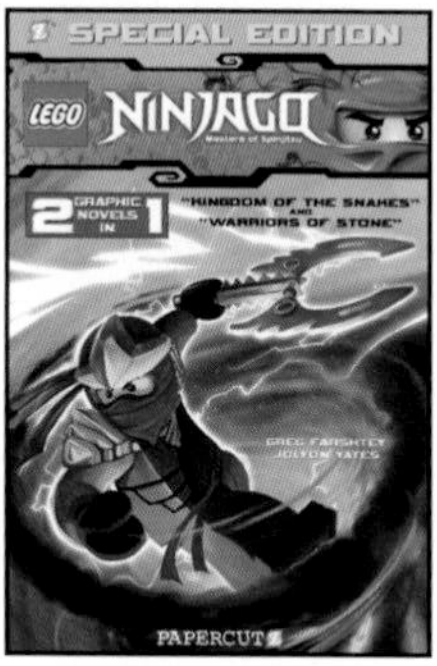
SPECIAL EDITION
LEGO NINJAGO
2 GRAPHIC NOVELS IN 1
"KINGDOM OF THE SNAKES"
"WARRIORS OF STONE"
GREG FARSHTEY
JOLYON YATES
PAPERCUTZ
SPECIAL EDITION #3
(Features stories from
NINJAGO #5 & #6.)

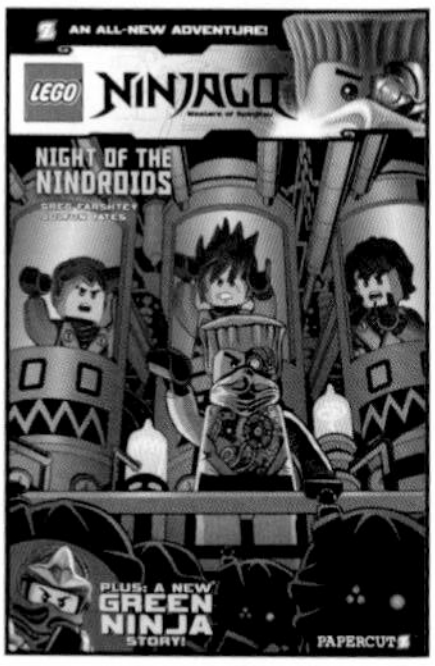
AN ALL-NEW ADVENTURE!
LEGO NINJAGO
NIGHT OF THE NINDROIDS
PLUS: A NEW GREEN NINJA STORY!
PAPERCUTZ
LEGO NINJAGO #9

LEGO® NINJAGO graphic novels are available in paperback and hardcover at booksellers everywhere.

LEGO® NINJAGO #1-10 are $6.99 in paperback, and $10.99 in hardcover. LEGO NINJAGO SPECIAL EDITION #1-3 are $10.99 in paperback only. You can also order online at papercutz.com. Or call 1-800-886-1223, Monday through Friday, 9 – 5 EST. MC, Visa, and AmEx accepted. To order by mail, please add $4.00 for postage and handling for first book ordered, $1.00 for each additional book and make check payable to NBM Publishing. Send to: Papercutz, 160 Broadway, Suite 700, East Wing, New York, NY 10038.

LEGO NINJAGO graphic novels are also available digitally wherever e-books are sold.

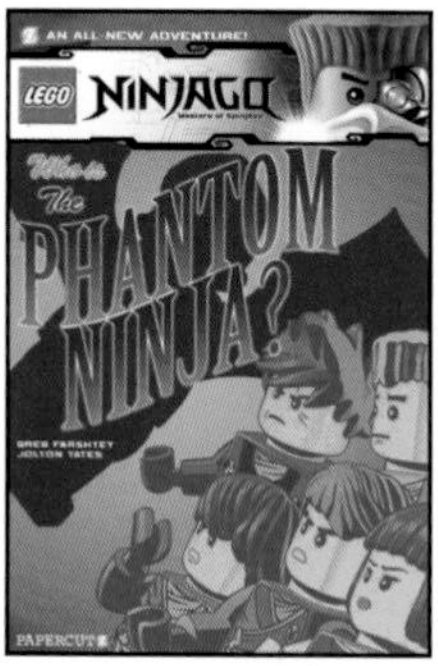
AN ALL-NEW ADVENTURE!
LEGO NINJAGO
Who is The PHANTOM NINJA?
GREG FARSHTEY
JOLYON YATES
PAPERCUTZ
LEGO NINJAGO #10

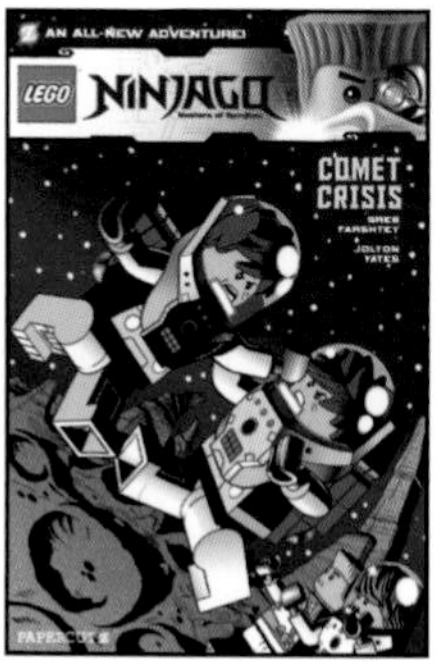
AN ALL-NEW ADVENTURE!
LEGO NINJAGO
COMET CRISIS
GREG FARSHTEY
JOLYON YATES
PAPERCUTZ
LEGO NINJAGO #11

LEGO NINJAGO
Masters of Spinjitzu

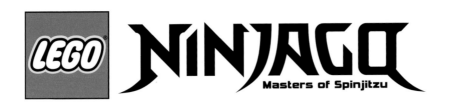

"COMET CRISIS"

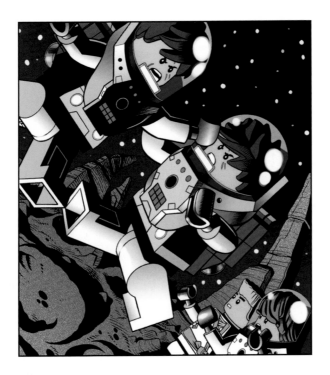

Greg Farshtey – Writer
Jolyon Yates – Artist
Laurie E. Smith – Colorist

PAPERCUTZ™
New York

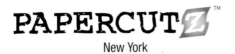

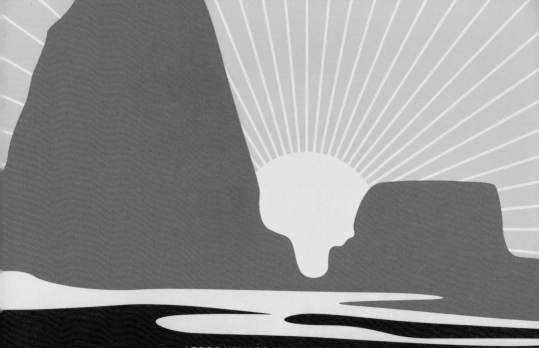

LEGO® NINJAGO Masters of Spinjitzu

#11 "Comet Crisis"

Greg Farshtey – Writer

Jolyon Yates – Artist

Laurie E. Smith – Colorist

Bryan Senka – Letterer

Dawn K. Guzzo – Production

Beth Scorzato – Production Coordinator

Michael Petranek – Associate Editor

Jim Salicrup
Editor-in-Chief

ISBN: 978-1-62991-046-8 paperback edition
ISBN: 978-1-62991-047-5 hardcover edition

Papercutz books may be purchased for business or promotional use. For information on bulk purchases please contact Macmillan Corporate and Premium Sales Department at (800) 221-7945 x5442.

Printed in Canada
August 2014 by Friesens
1 Printers Way
Altona, MB R0G 0B0

FSC
www.fsc.org
MIX
Paper from responsible sources
FSC® C016245

Distributed by Macmillan
First Printing

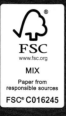

MEET THE MASTERS OF SPINJITZU

JAY

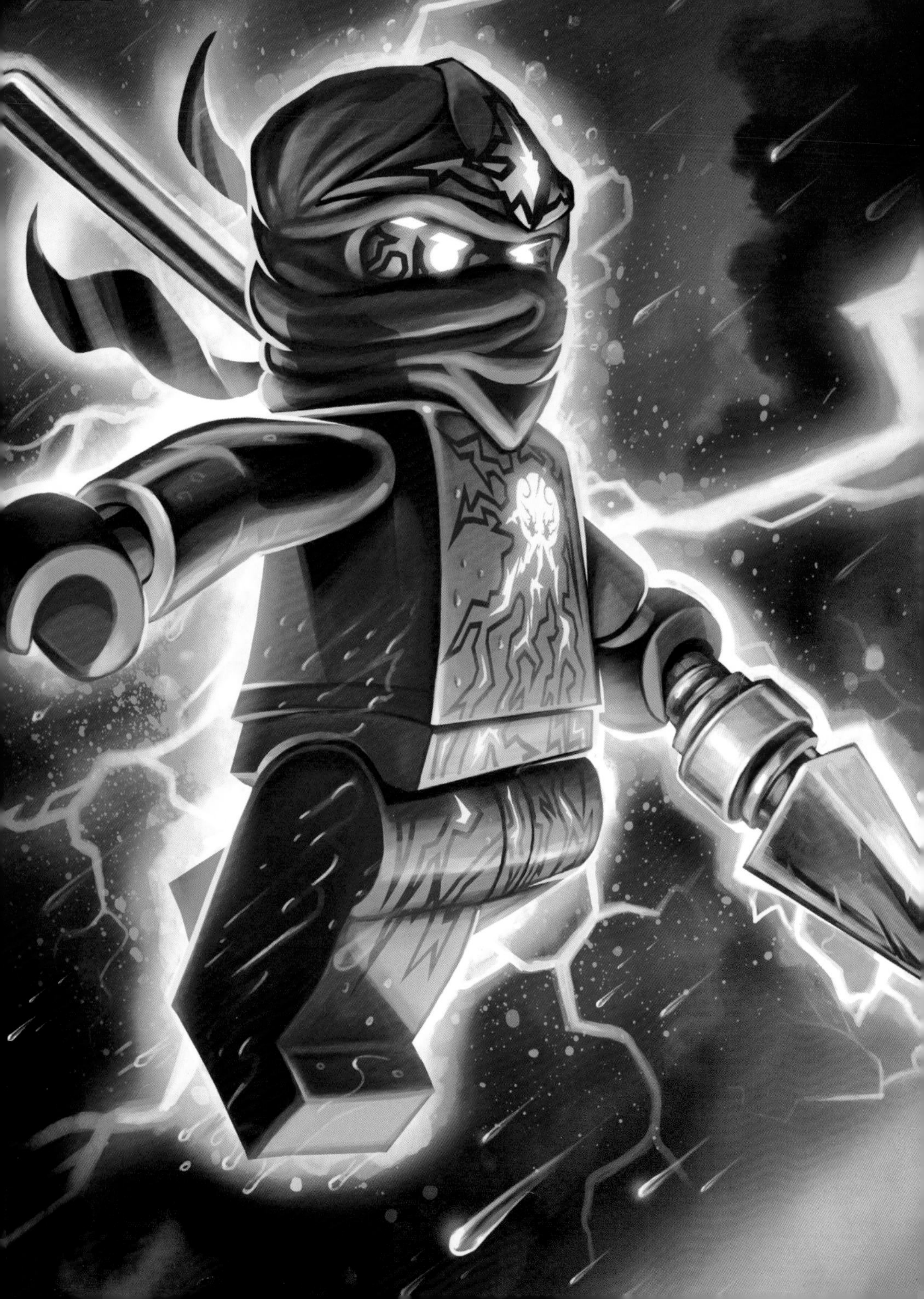

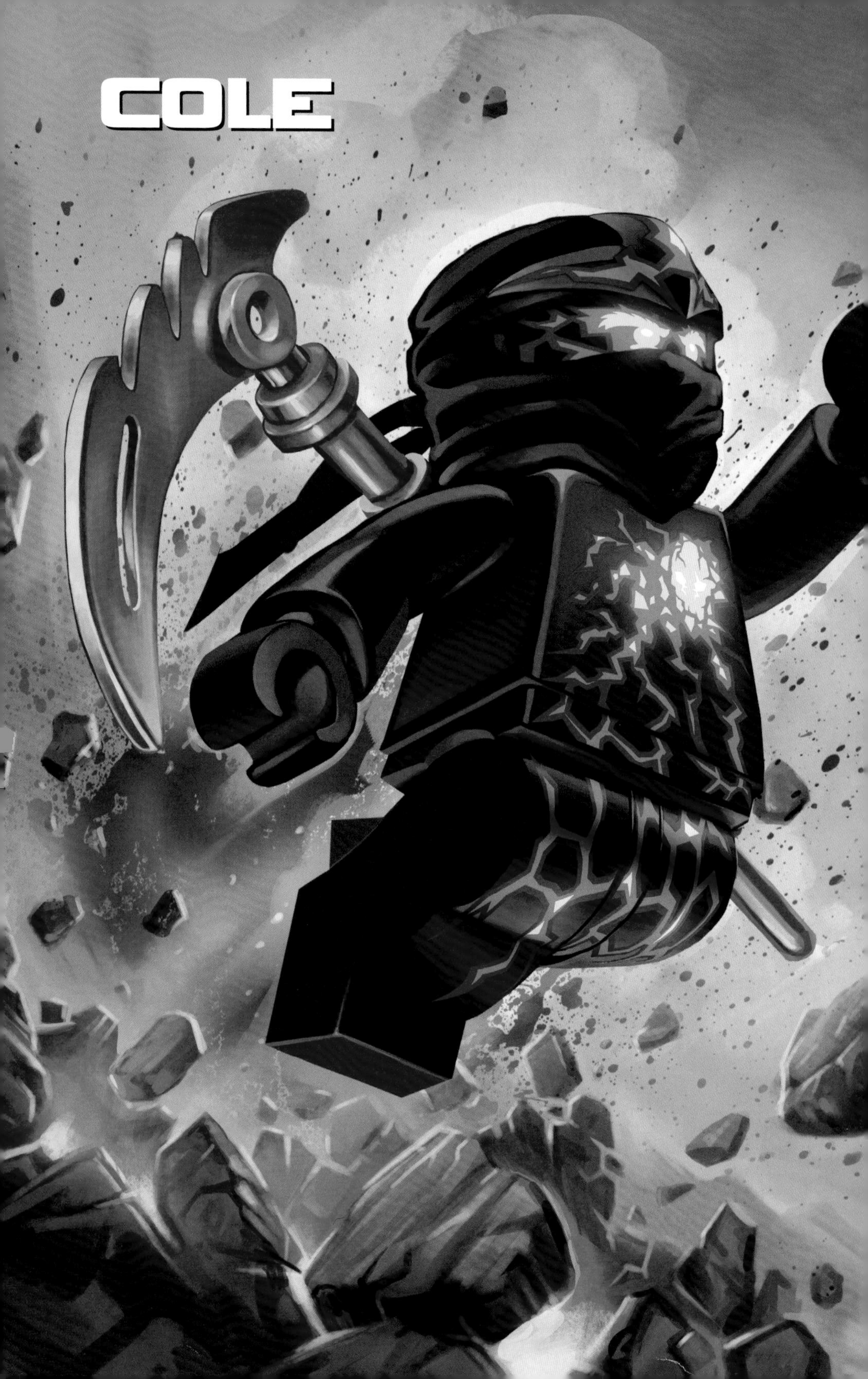
COLE

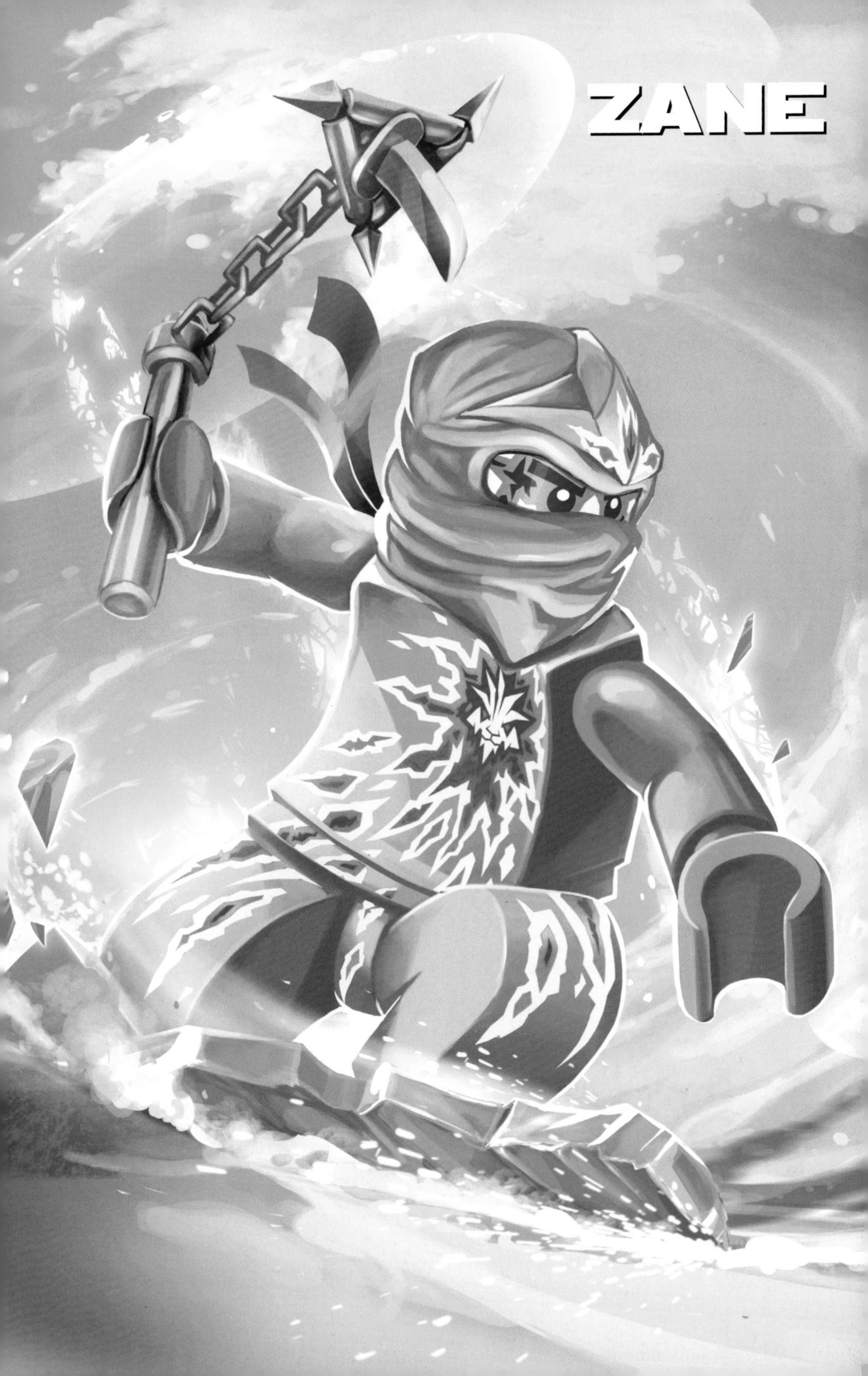
ZANE

KAI

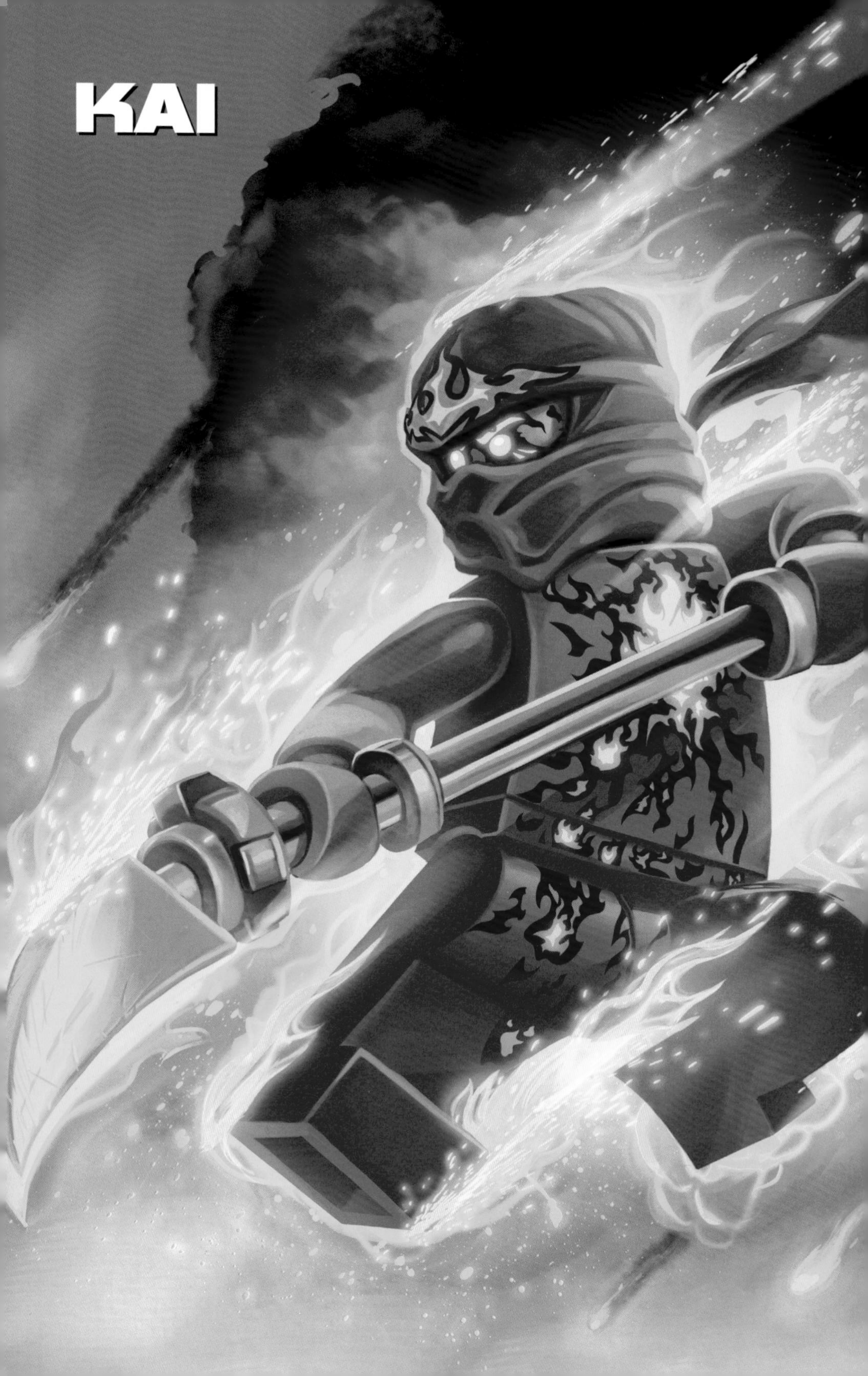

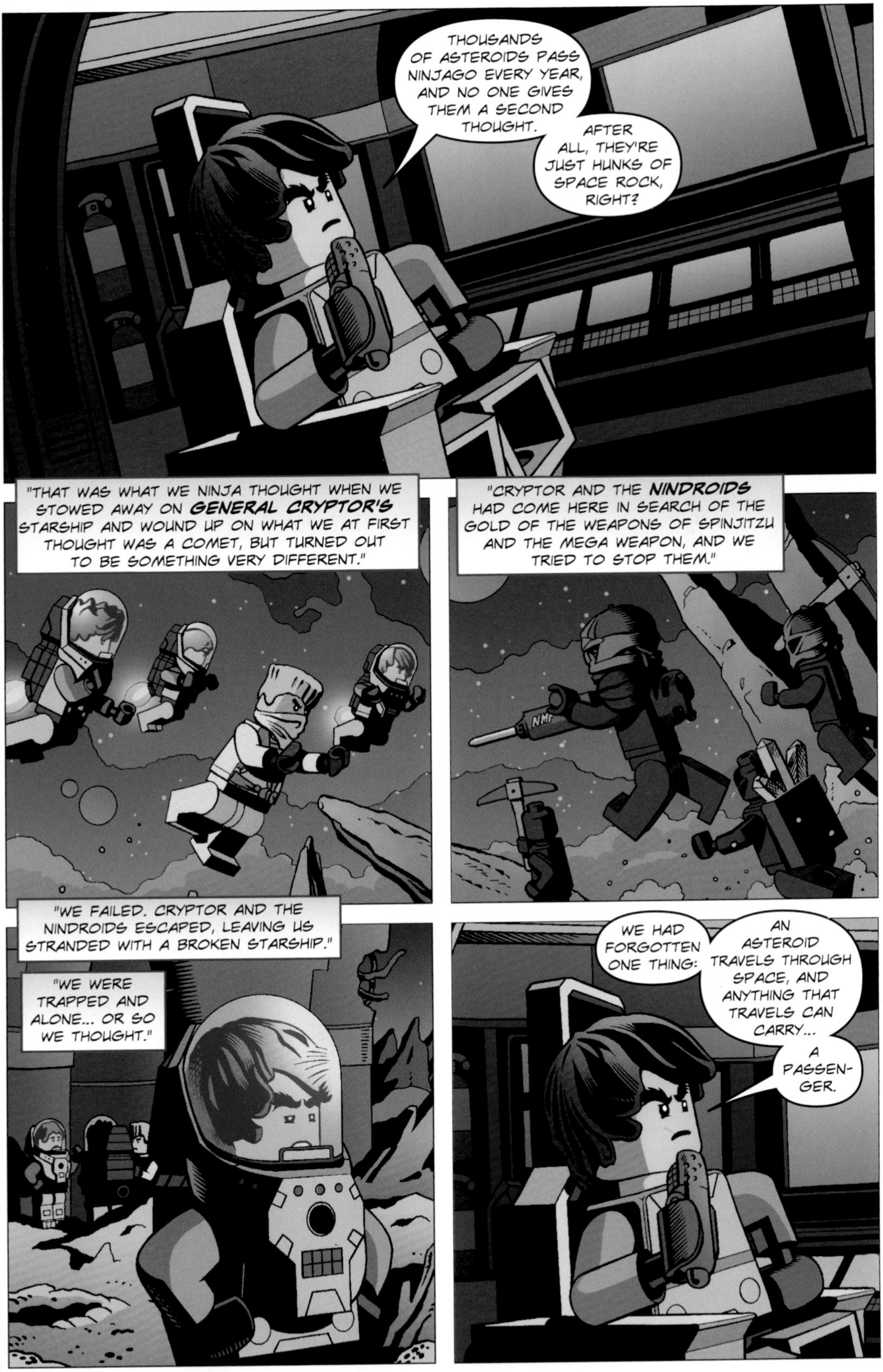
THOUSANDS OF ASTEROIDS PASS NINJAGO EVERY YEAR, AND NO ONE GIVES THEM A SECOND THOUGHT.
AFTER ALL, THEY'RE JUST HUNKS OF SPACE ROCK, RIGHT?
"THAT WAS WHAT WE NINJA THOUGHT WHEN WE STOWED AWAY ON GENERAL CRYPTOR'S STARSHIP AND WOUND UP ON WHAT WE AT FIRST THOUGHT WAS A COMET, BUT TURNED OUT TO BE SOMETHING VERY DIFFERENT."
"CRYPTOR AND THE NINDROIDS HAD COME HERE IN SEARCH OF THE GOLD OF THE WEAPONS OF SPINJITZU AND THE MEGA WEAPON, AND WE TRIED TO STOP THEM."
"WE FAILED. CRYPTOR AND THE NINDROIDS ESCAPED, LEAVING US STRANDED WITH A BROKEN STARSHIP."
"WE WERE TRAPPED AND ALONE... OR SO WE THOUGHT."
WE HAD FORGOTTEN ONE THING:
AN ASTEROID TRAVELS THROUGH SPACE, AND ANYTHING THAT TRAVELS CAN CARRY...
A PASSEN-GER.

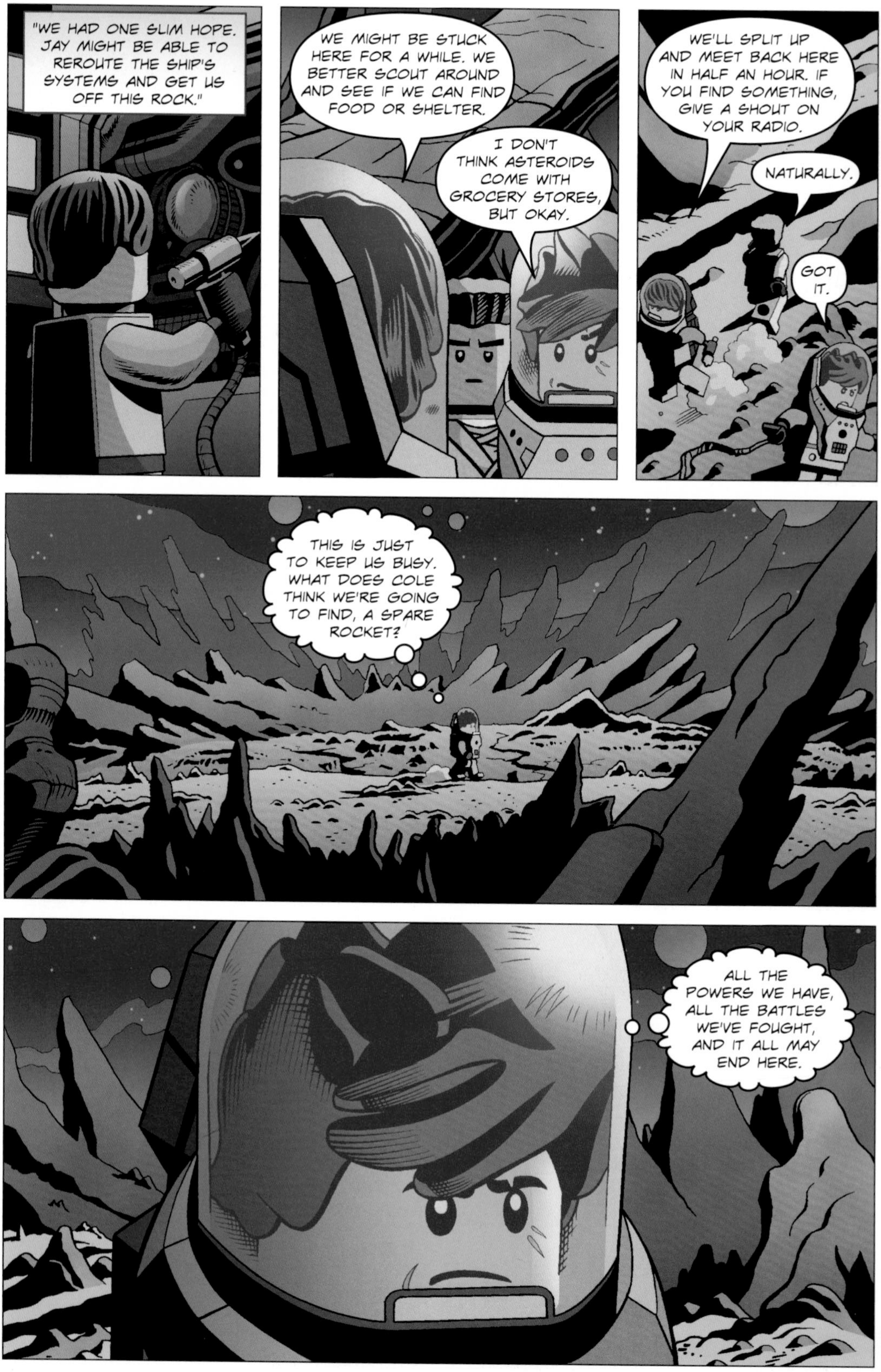
"WE HAD ONE SLIM HOPE. JAY MIGHT BE ABLE TO REROUTE THE SHIP'S SYSTEMS AND GET US OFF THIS ROCK."
WE MIGHT BE STUCK HERE FOR A WHILE. WE BETTER SCOUT AROUND AND SEE IF WE CAN FIND FOOD OR SHELTER.
I DON'T THINK ASTEROIDS COME WITH GROCERY STORES, BUT OKAY.
WE'LL SPLIT UP AND MEET BACK HERE IN HALF AN HOUR. IF YOU FIND SOMETHING, GIVE A SHOUT ON YOUR RADIO.
NATURALLY.
GOT IT.
THIS IS JUST TO KEEP US BUSY. WHAT DOES COLE THINK WE'RE GOING TO FIND, A SPARE ROCKET?
ALL THE POWERS WE HAVE, ALL THE BATTLES WE'VE FOUGHT, AND IT ALL MAY END HERE.

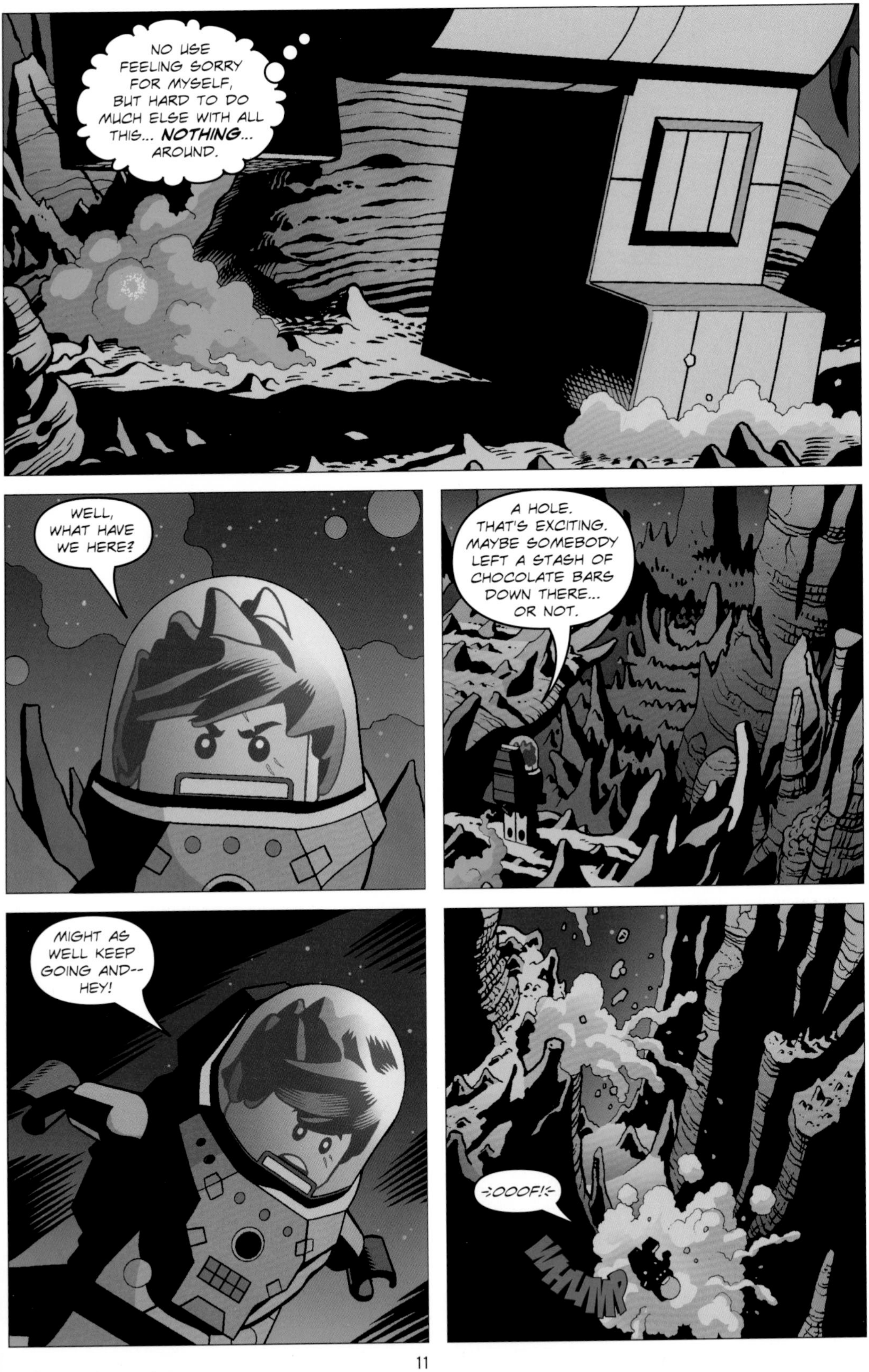
NO USE FEELING SORRY FOR MYSELF, BUT HARD TO DO MUCH ELSE WITH ALL THIS... NOTHING... AROUND.
WELL, WHAT HAVE WE HERE?
A HOLE. THAT'S EXCITING. MAYBE SOMEBODY LEFT A STASH OF CHOCOLATE BARS DOWN THERE... OR NOT.
MIGHT AS WELL KEEP GOING AND-- HEY!
OOOF!
WHUMP

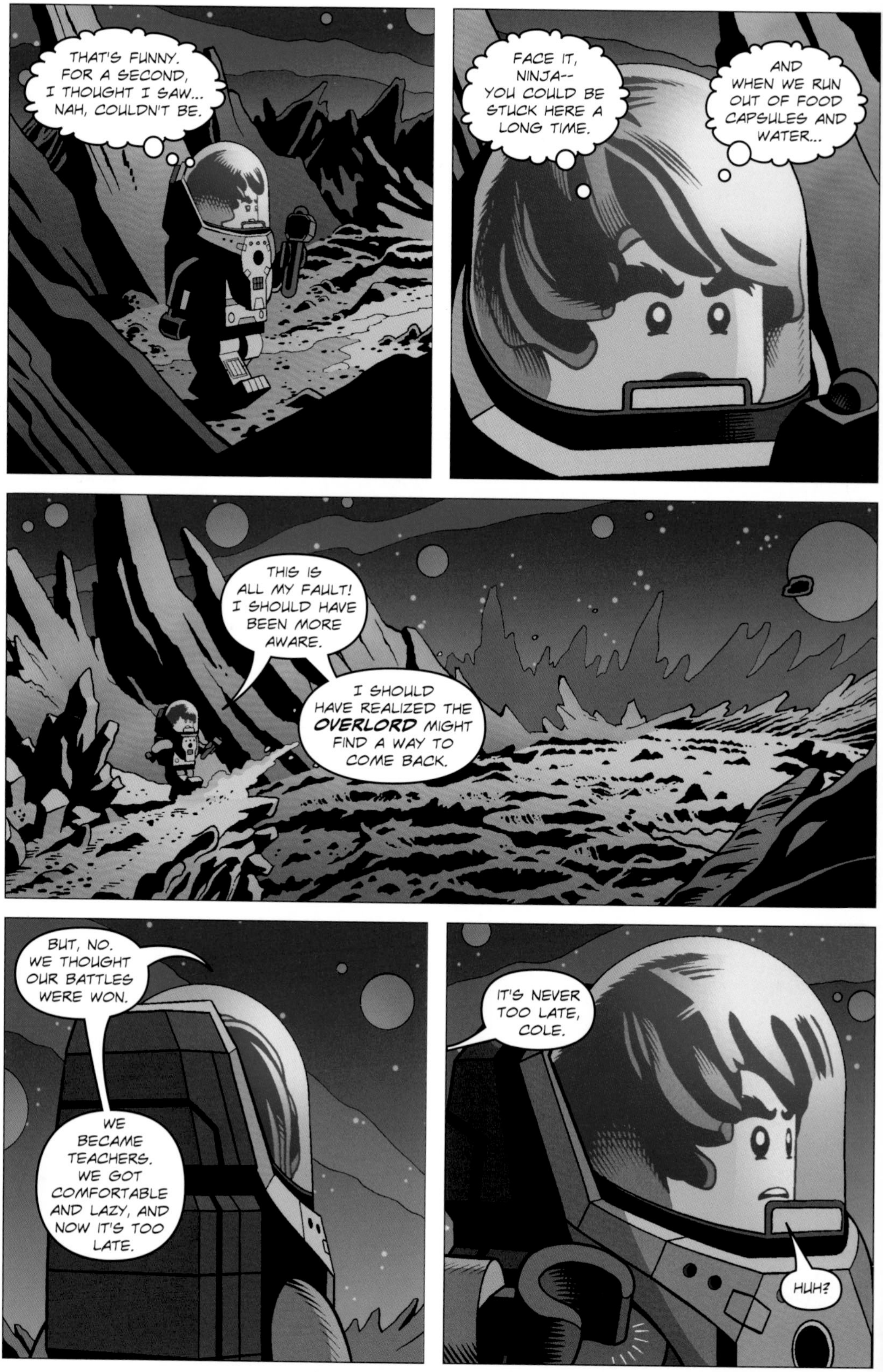
THAT'S FUNNY. FOR A SECOND, I THOUGHT I SAW... NAH, COULDN'T BE.
FACE IT, NINJA-- YOU COULD BE STUCK HERE A LONG TIME.
AND WHEN WE RUN OUT OF FOOD CAPSULES AND WATER...
THIS IS ALL MY FAULT! I SHOULD HAVE BEEN MORE AWARE.
I SHOULD HAVE REALIZED THE OVERLORD MIGHT FIND A WAY TO COME BACK.
BUT, NO. WE THOUGHT OUR BATTLES WERE WON.
WE BECAME TEACHERS. WE GOT COMFORTABLE AND LAZY, AND NOW IT'S TOO LATE.
IT'S NEVER TOO LATE, COLE.
HUH?

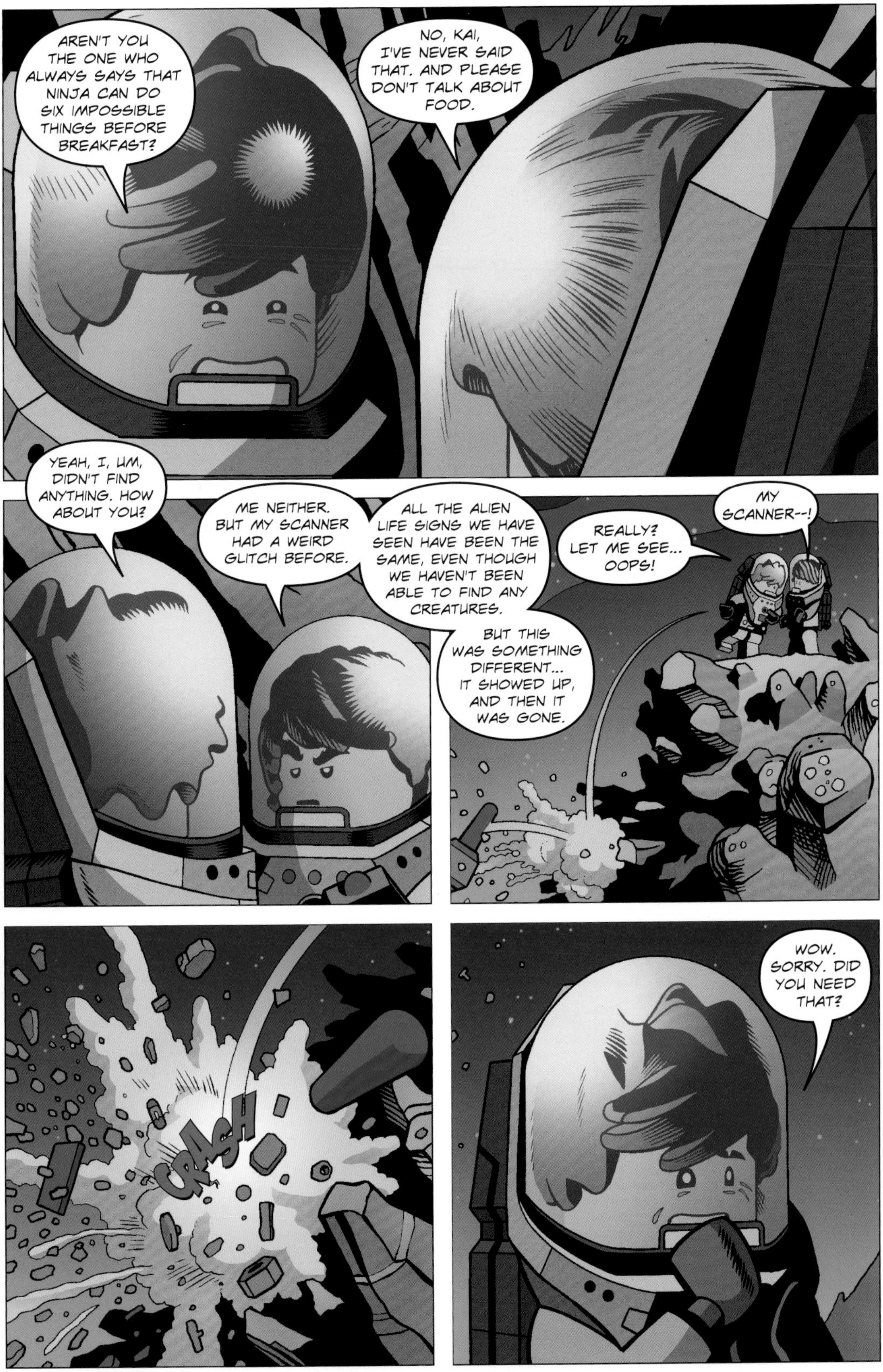
AREN'T YOU THE ONE WHO ALWAYS SAYS THAT NINJA CAN DO SIX IMPOSSIBLE THINGS BEFORE BREAKFAST?
NO, KAI, I'VE NEVER SAID THAT. AND PLEASE DON'T TALK ABOUT FOOD.
YEAH, I, UM, DIDN'T FIND ANYTHING. HOW ABOUT YOU?
ME NEITHER. BUT MY SCANNER HAD A WEIRD GLITCH BEFORE.
ALL THE ALIEN LIFE SIGNS WE HAVE SEEN HAVE BEEN THE SAME, EVEN THOUGH WE HAVEN'T BEEN ABLE TO FIND ANY CREATURES.
BUT THIS WAS SOMETHING DIFFERENT... IT SHOWED UP, AND THEN IT WAS GONE.
REALLY? LET ME SEE... OOPS!
MY SCANNER--!
CRASH
WOW. SORRY. DID YOU NEED THAT?

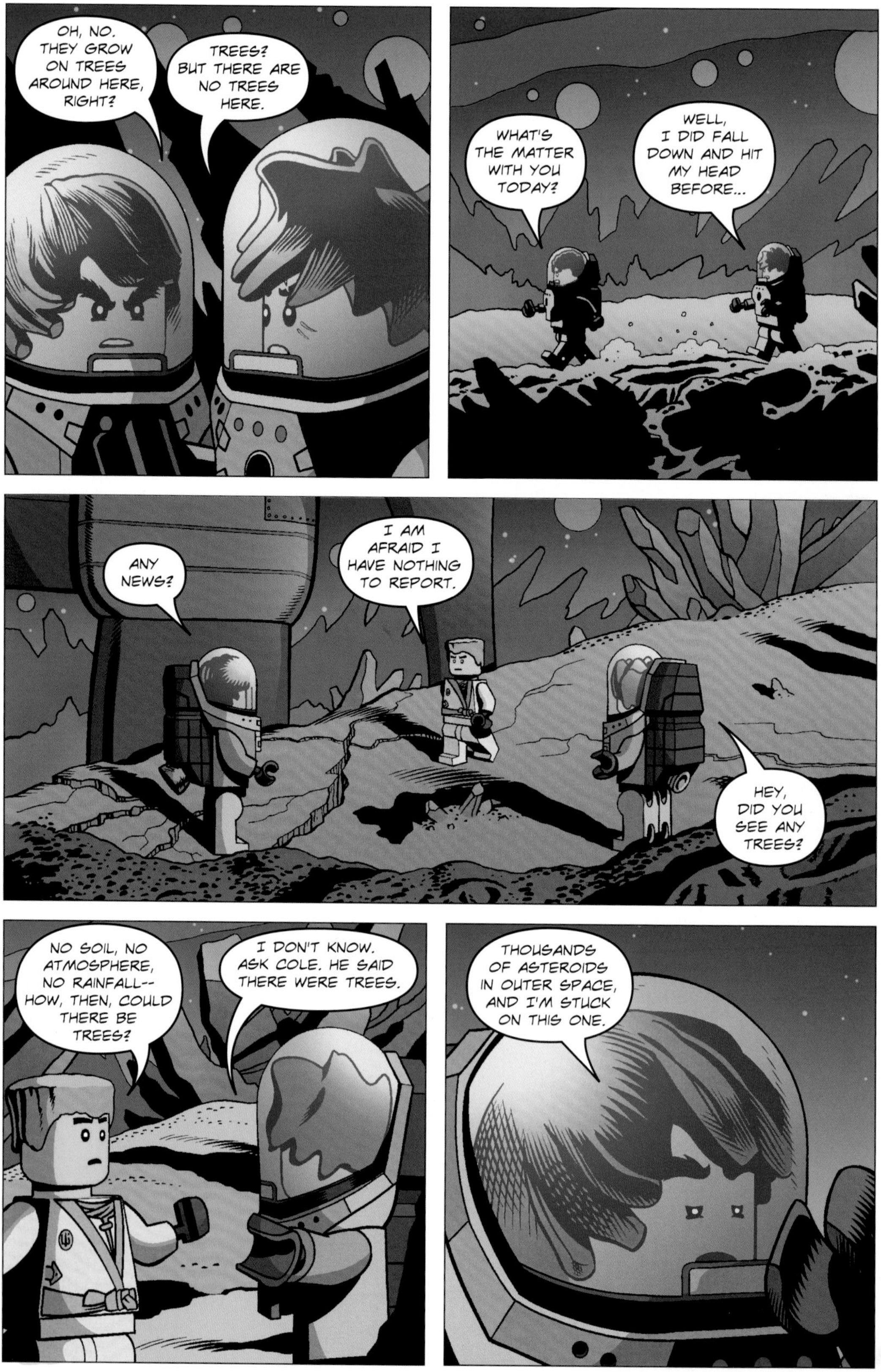
OH, NO. THEY GROW ON TREES AROUND HERE, RIGHT?
TREES? BUT THERE ARE NO TREES HERE.
WHAT'S THE MATTER WITH YOU TODAY?
WELL, I DID FALL DOWN AND HIT MY HEAD BEFORE...
ANY NEWS?
I AM AFRAID I HAVE NOTHING TO REPORT.
HEY, DID YOU SEE ANY TREES?
NO SOIL, NO ATMOSPHERE, NO RAINFALL-- HOW, THEN, COULD THERE BE TREES?
I DON'T KNOW. ASK COLE. HE SAID THERE WERE TREES.
THOUSANDS OF ASTEROIDS IN OUTER SPACE, AND I'M STUCK ON THIS ONE.

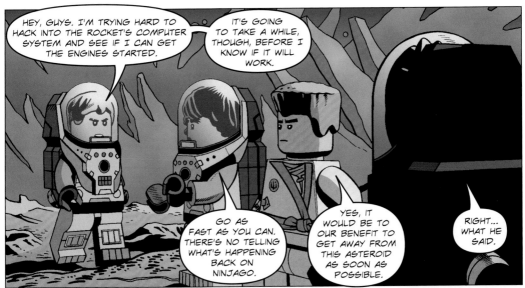

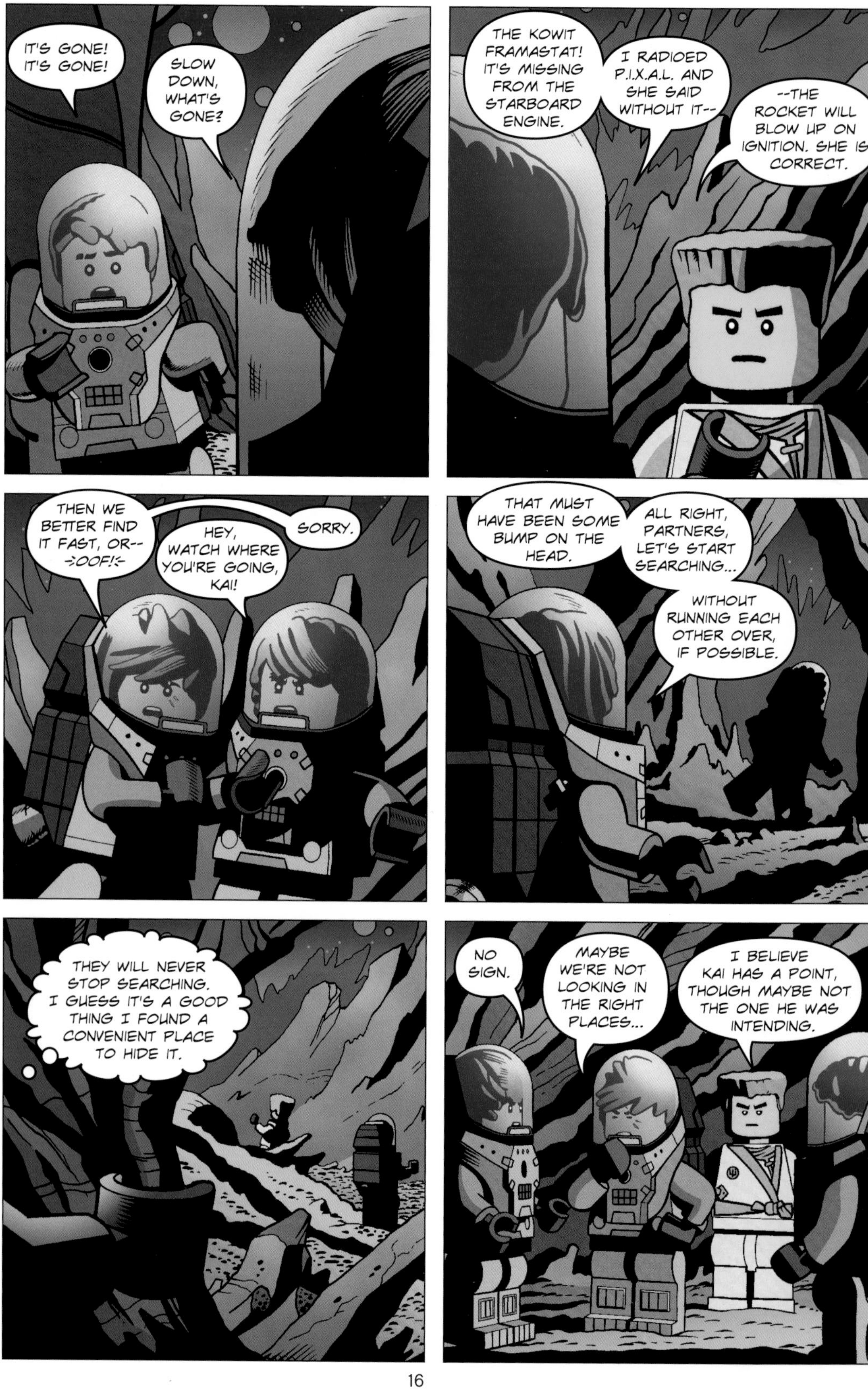
IT'S GONE! IT'S GONE!
SLOW DOWN, WHAT'S GONE?
THE KOWIT FRAMASTAT! IT'S MISSING FROM THE STARBOARD ENGINE.
I RADIOED P.I.X.A.L. AND SHE SAID WITHOUT IT--
--THE ROCKET WILL BLOW UP ON IGNITION. SHE IS CORRECT.
THEN WE BETTER FIND IT FAST, OR-- ->OOF!<-
HEY, WATCH WHERE YOU'RE GOING, KAI!
SORRY.
THAT MUST HAVE BEEN SOME BUMP ON THE HEAD.
ALL RIGHT, PARTNERS, LET'S START SEARCHING...
WITHOUT RUNNING EACH OTHER OVER, IF POSSIBLE.
THEY WILL NEVER STOP SEARCHING. I GUESS IT'S A GOOD THING I FOUND A CONVENIENT PLACE TO HIDE IT.
NO SIGN.
MAYBE WE'RE NOT LOOKING IN THE RIGHT PLACES...
I BELIEVE KAI HAS A POINT, THOUGH MAYBE NOT THE ONE HE WAS INTENDING.

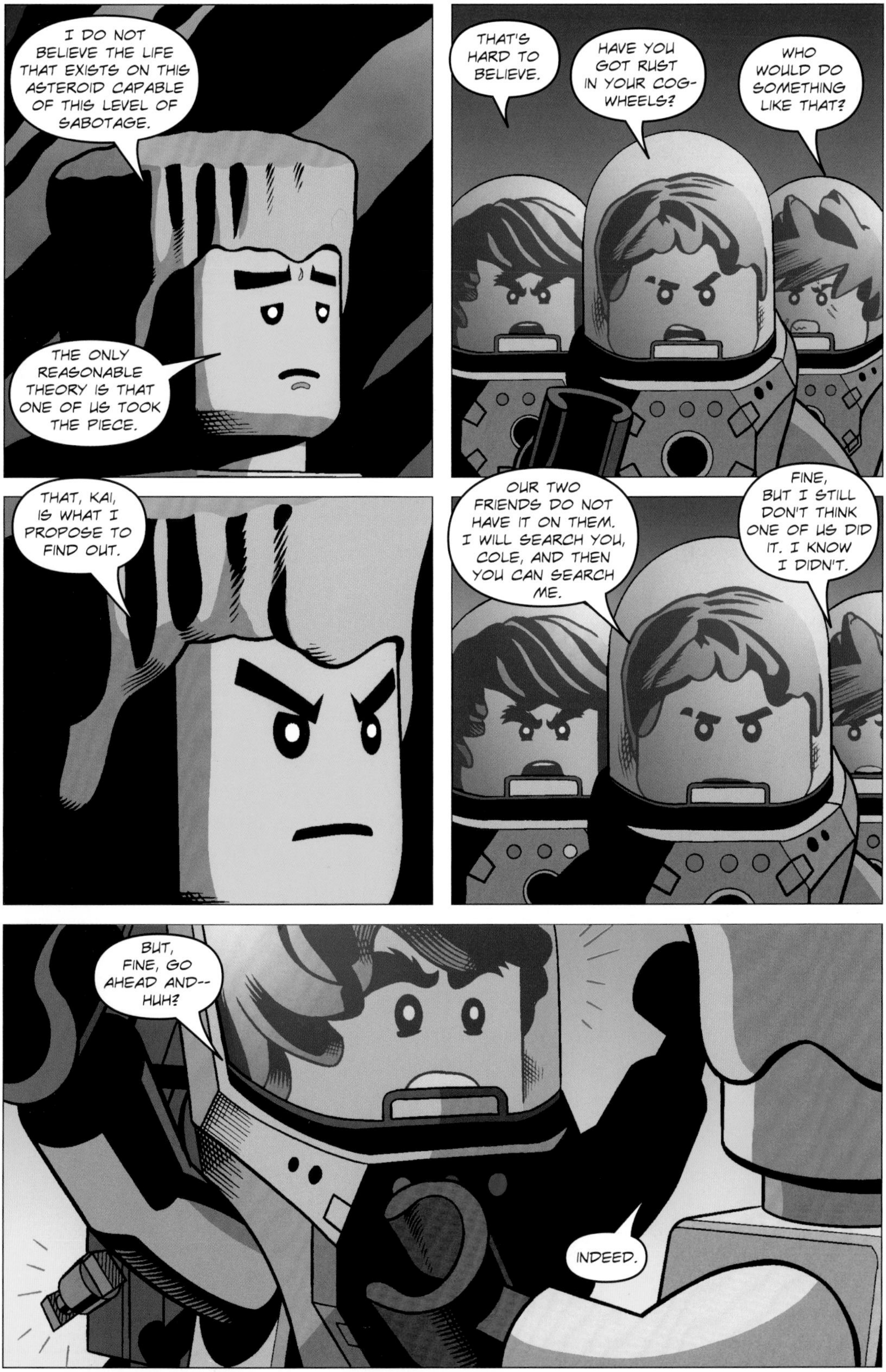
I DO NOT BELIEVE THE LIFE THAT EXISTS ON THIS ASTEROID CAPABLE OF THIS LEVEL OF SABOTAGE.
THE ONLY REASONABLE THEORY IS THAT ONE OF US TOOK THE PIECE.
THAT'S HARD TO BELIEVE.
HAVE YOU GOT RUST IN YOUR COG-WHEELS?
WHO WOULD DO SOMETHING LIKE THAT?
THAT, KAI, IS WHAT I PROPOSE TO FIND OUT.
OUR TWO FRIENDS DO NOT HAVE IT ON THEM. I WILL SEARCH YOU, COLE, AND THEN YOU CAN SEARCH ME.
FINE, BUT I STILL DON'T THINK ONE OF US DID IT. I KNOW I DIDN'T.
BUT, FINE, GO AHEAD AND-- HUH?
INDEED.

18

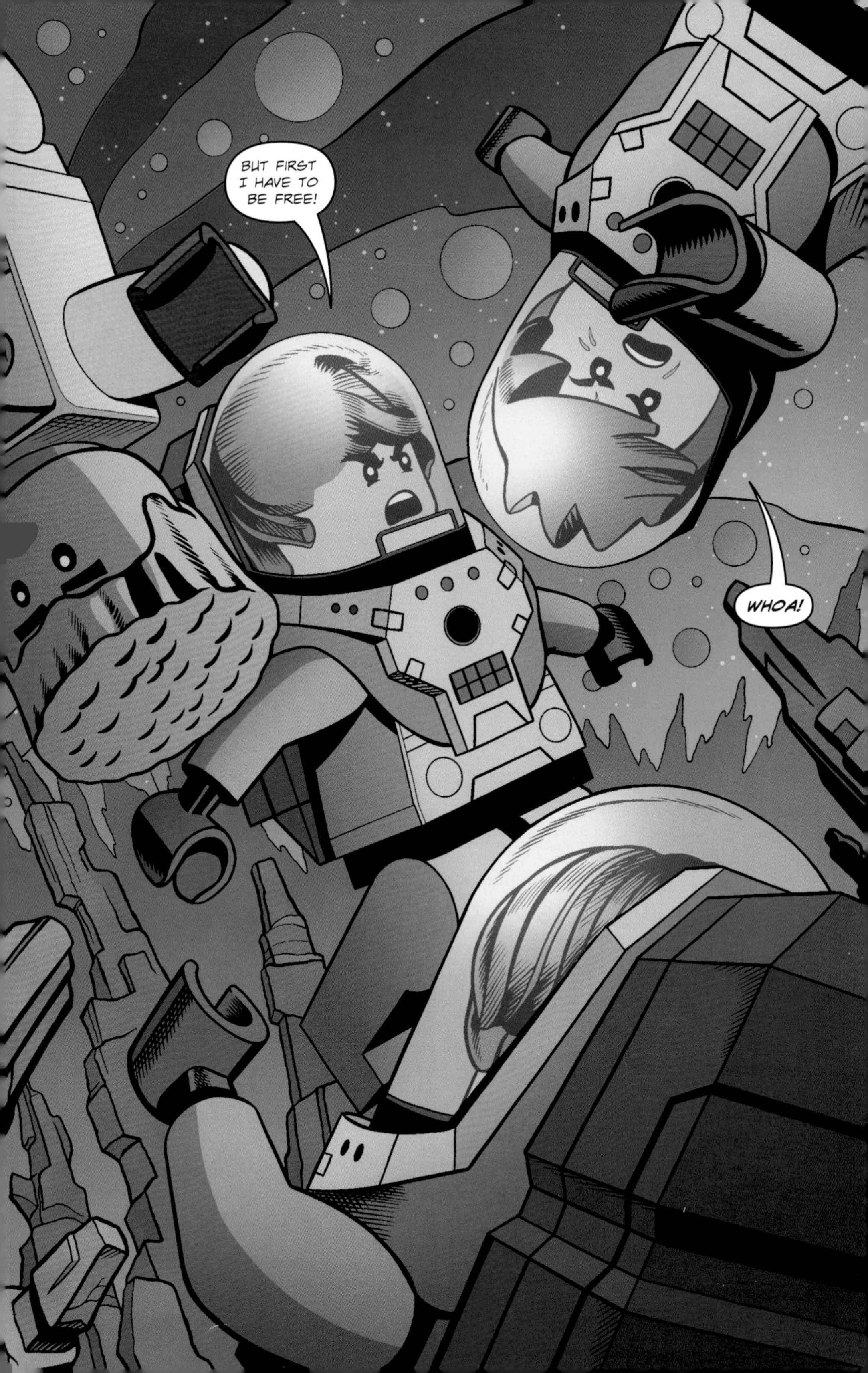
BUT FIRST I HAVE TO BE FREE!
WHOA!

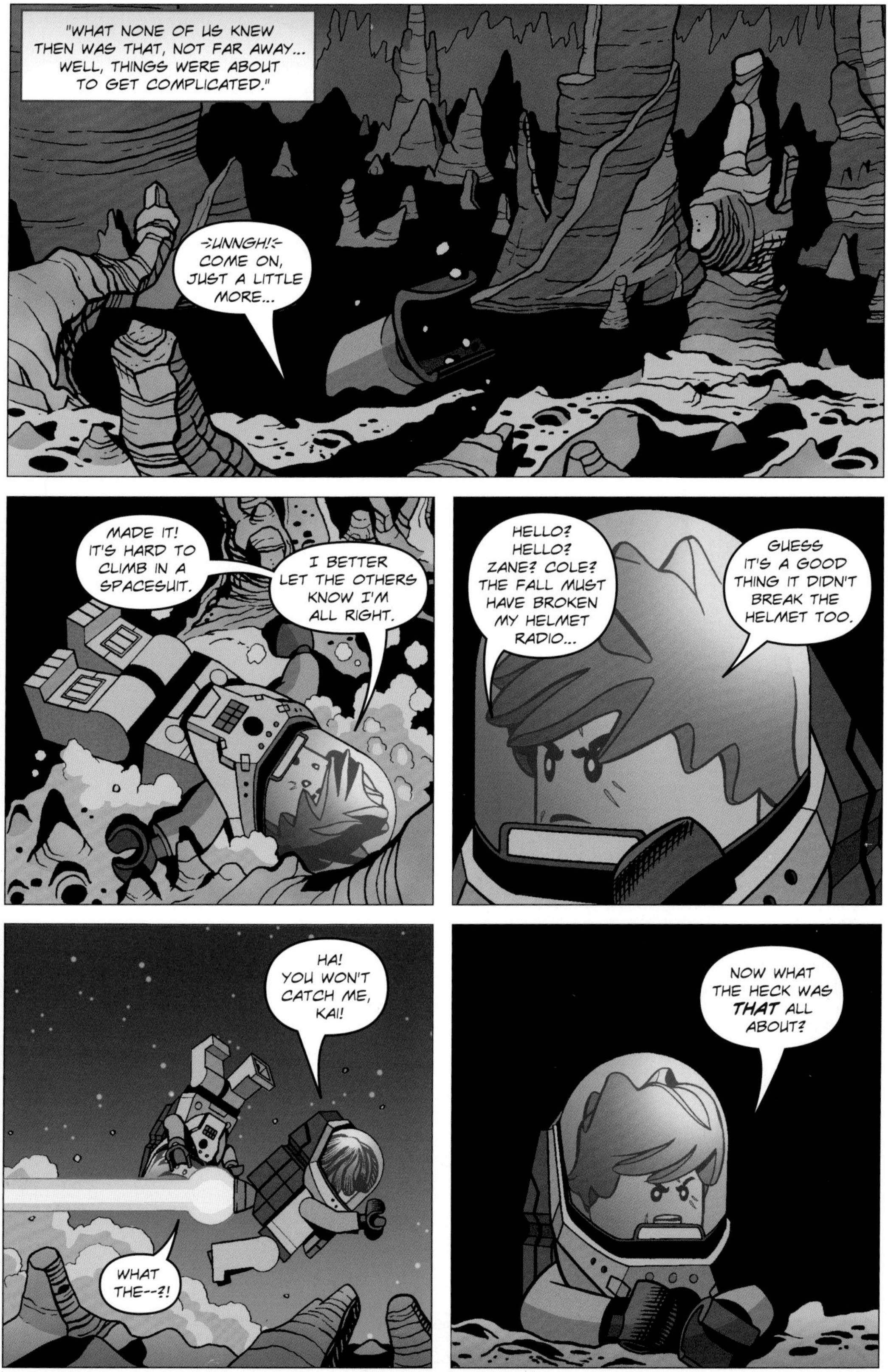
"WHAT NONE OF US KNEW THEN WAS THAT, NOT FAR AWAY... WELL, THINGS WERE ABOUT TO GET COMPLICATED."
-UNNGH!- COME ON, JUST A LITTLE MORE...
MADE IT! IT'S HARD TO CLIMB IN A SPACESUIT.
I BETTER LET THE OTHERS KNOW I'M ALL RIGHT.
HELLO? HELLO? ZANE? COLE? THE FALL MUST HAVE BROKEN MY HELMET RADIO...
GUESS IT'S A GOOD THING IT DIDN'T BREAK THE HELMET TOO.
HA! YOU WON'T CATCH ME, KAI!
WHAT THE--?!
NOW WHAT THE HECK WAS *THAT* ALL ABOUT?

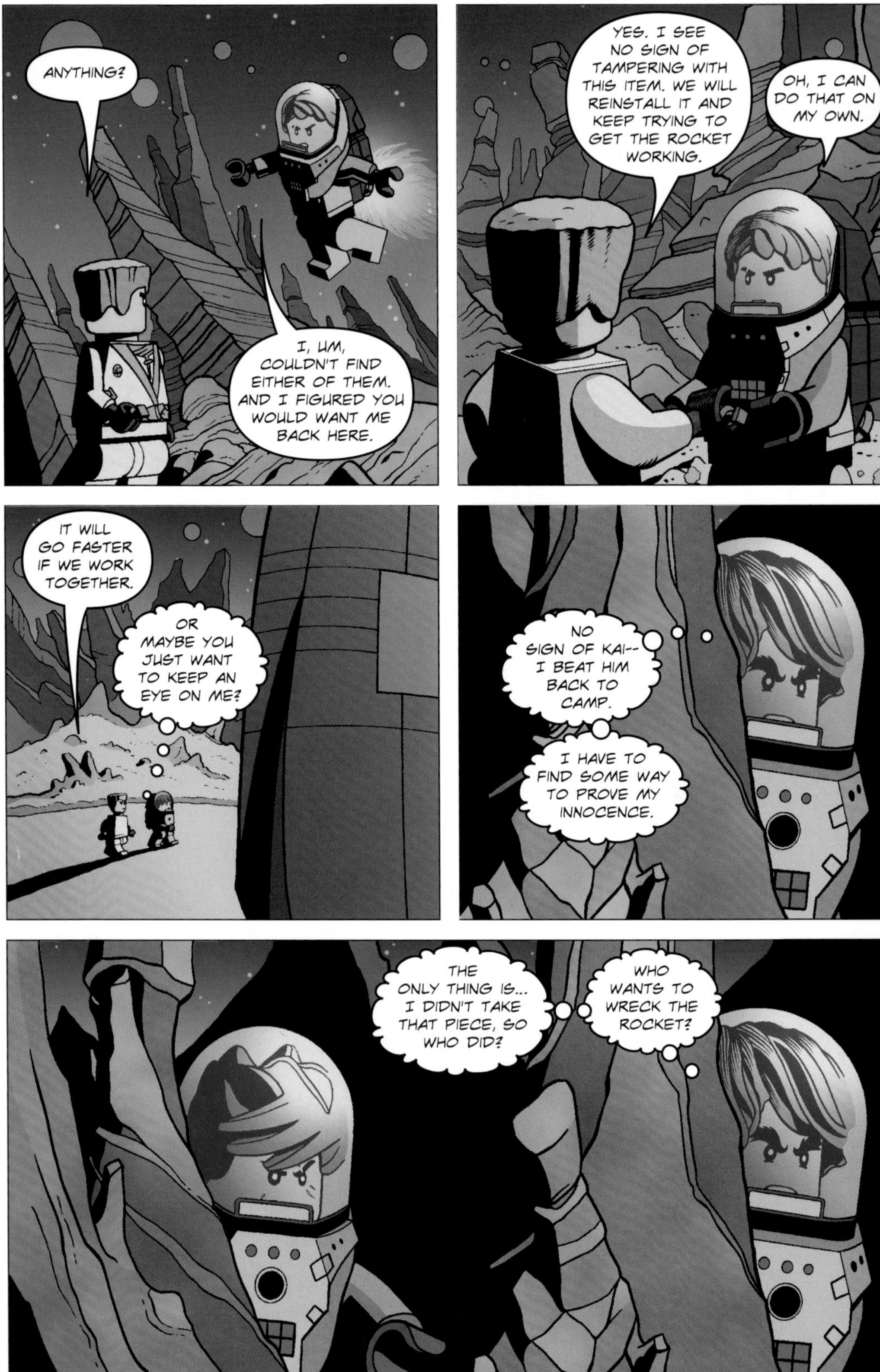
ANYTHING?
I, UM, COULDN'T FIND EITHER OF THEM. AND I FIGURED YOU WOULD WANT ME BACK HERE.
YES. I SEE NO SIGN OF TAMPERING WITH THIS ITEM. WE WILL REINSTALL IT AND KEEP TRYING TO GET THE ROCKET WORKING.
OH, I CAN DO THAT ON MY OWN.
IT WILL GO FASTER IF WE WORK TOGETHER.
OR MAYBE YOU JUST WANT TO KEEP AN EYE ON ME?
NO SIGN OF KAI-- I BEAT HIM BACK TO CAMP.
I HAVE TO FIND SOME WAY TO PROVE MY INNOCENCE.
THE ONLY THING IS... I DIDN'T TAKE THAT PIECE, SO WHO DID?
WHO WANTS TO WRECK THE ROCKET?

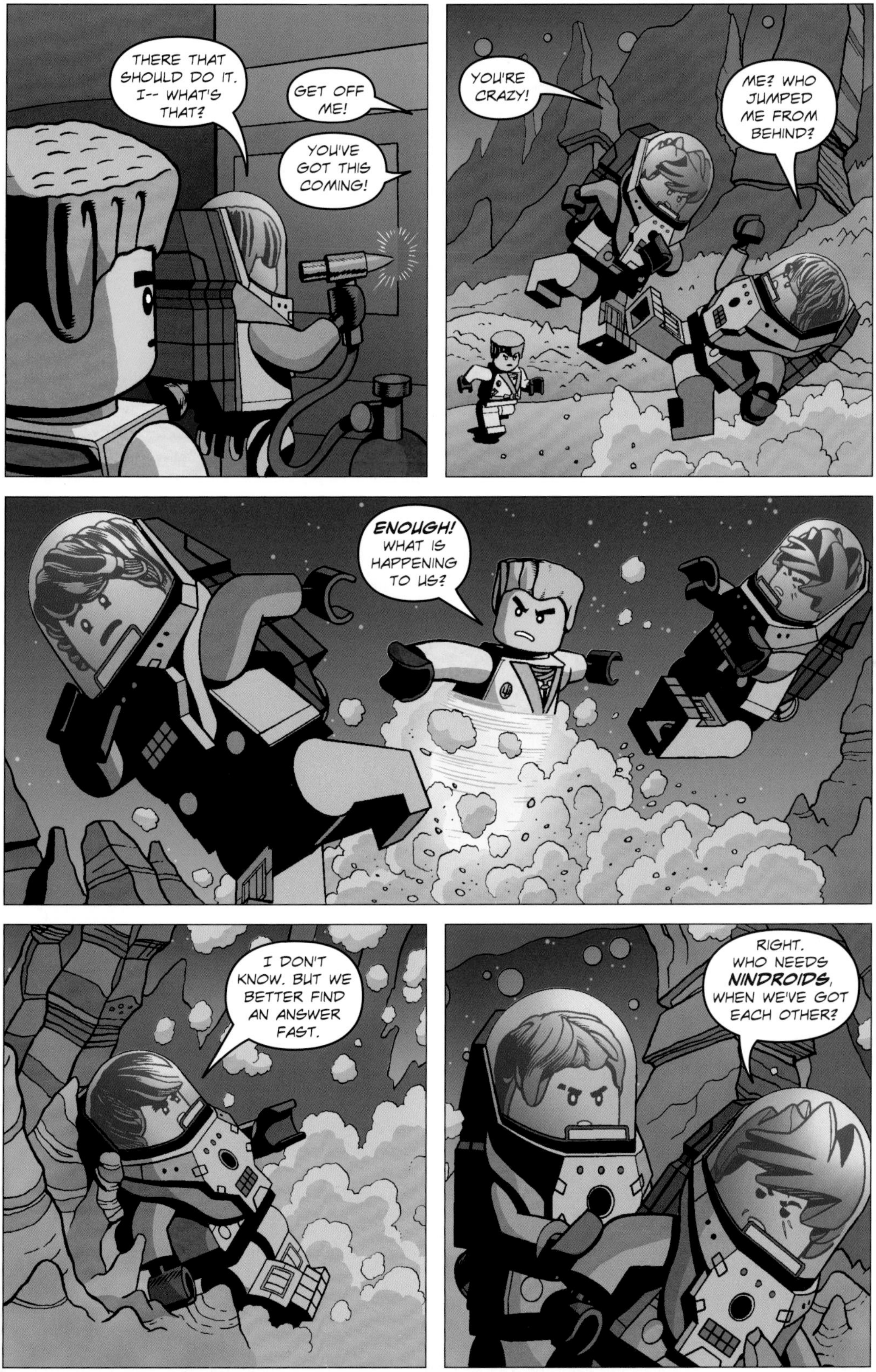
THERE THAT SHOULD DO IT. I-- WHAT'S THAT?
GET OFF ME!
YOU'VE GOT THIS COMING!
YOU'RE CRAZY!
ME? WHO JUMPED ME FROM BEHIND?
ENOUGH! WHAT IS HAPPENING TO US?
I DON'T KNOW. BUT WE BETTER FIND AN ANSWER FAST.
RIGHT. WHO NEEDS **NINDROIDS**, WHEN WE'VE GOT EACH OTHER?

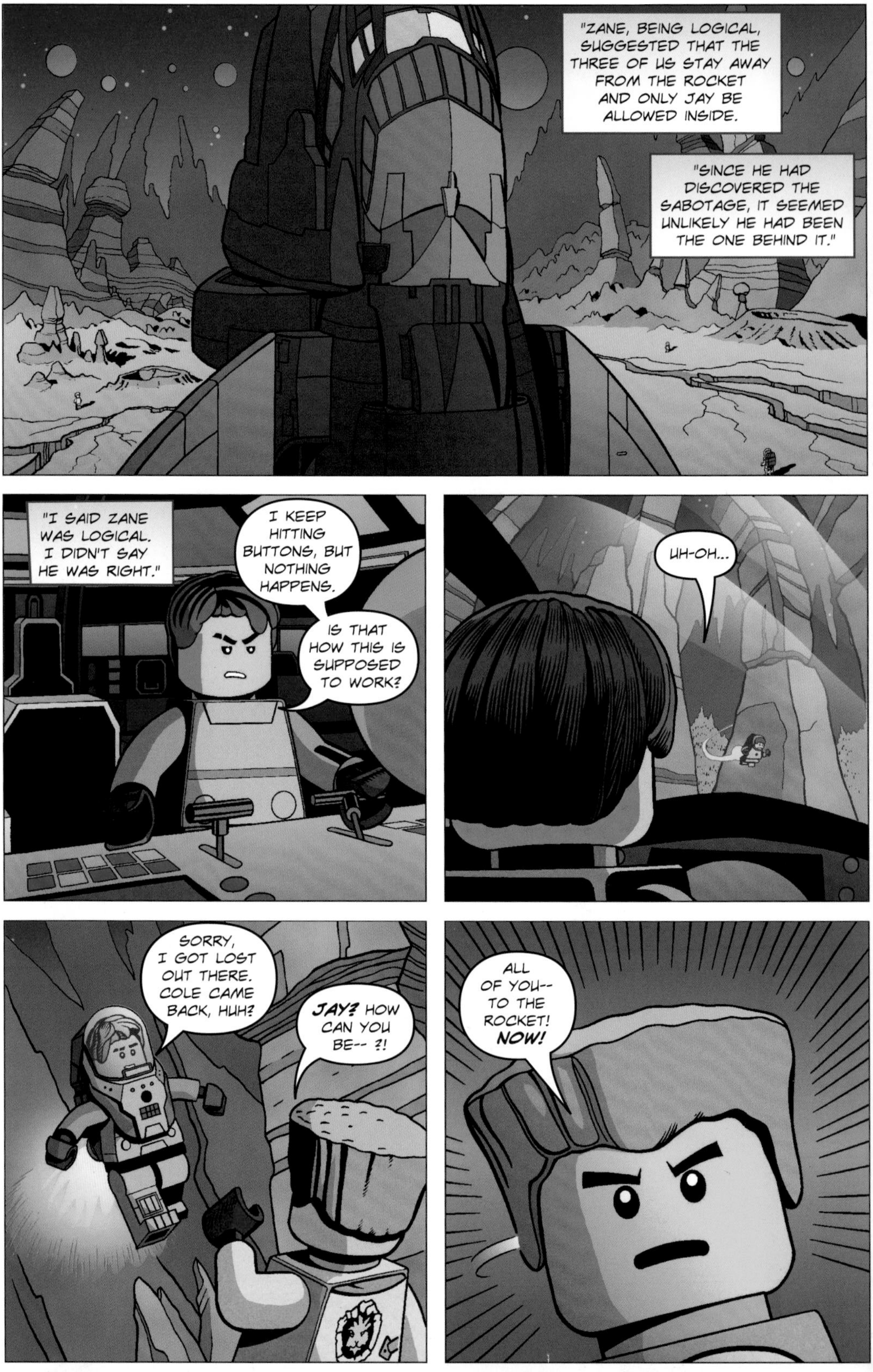
"ZANE, BEING LOGICAL, SUGGESTED THAT THE THREE OF US STAY AWAY FROM THE ROCKET AND ONLY JAY BE ALLOWED INSIDE.
"SINCE HE HAD DISCOVERED THE SABOTAGE, IT SEEMED UNLIKELY HE HAD BEEN THE ONE BEHIND IT."
"I SAID ZANE WAS LOGICAL. I DIDN'T SAY HE WAS RIGHT."
I KEEP HITTING BUTTONS, BUT NOTHING HAPPENS.
IS THAT HOW THIS IS SUPPOSED TO WORK?
UH-OH...
SORRY, I GOT LOST OUT THERE. COLE CAME BACK, HUH?
JAY? HOW CAN YOU BE-- ?!
ALL OF YOU-- TO THE ROCKET! NOW!

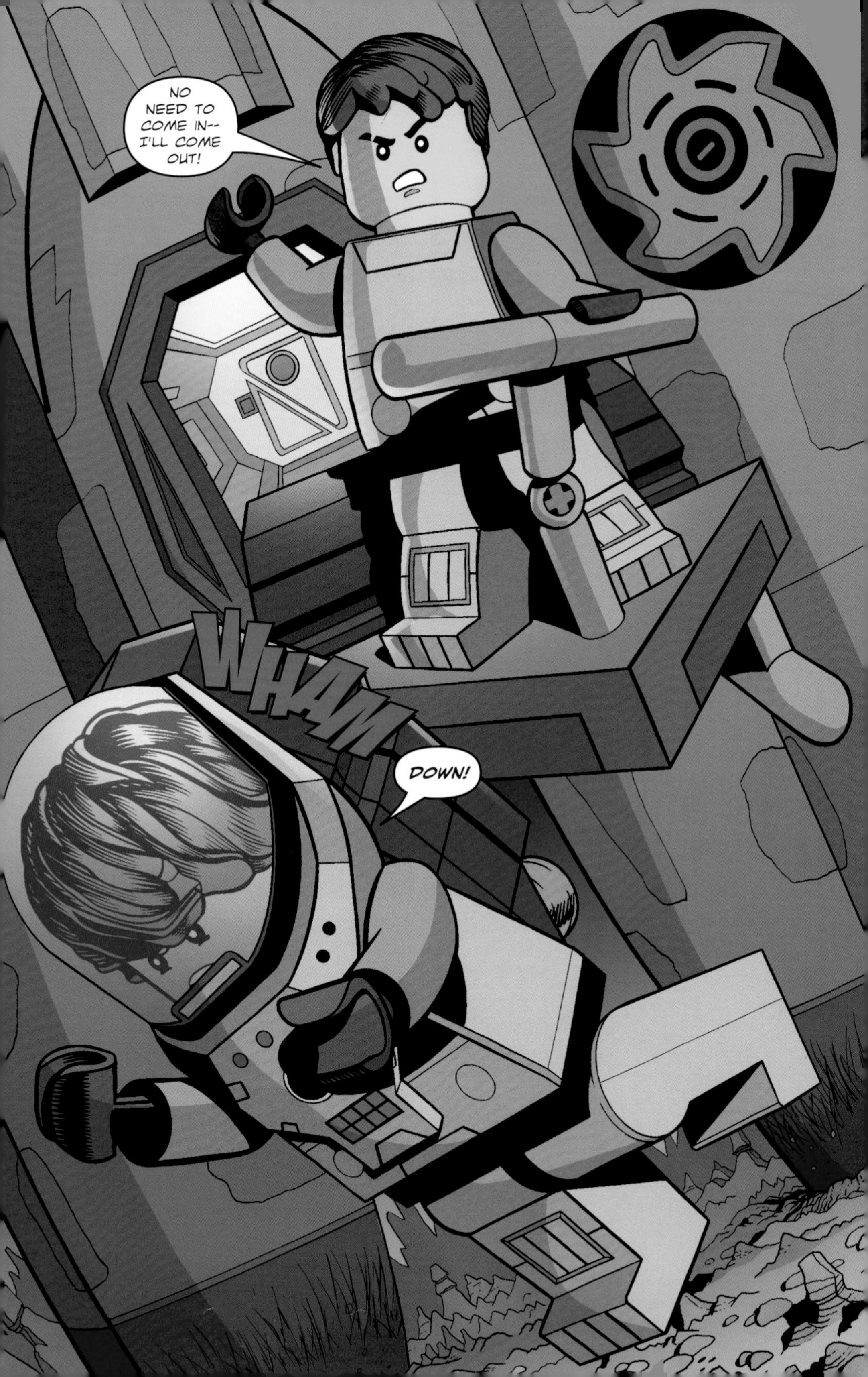
NO NEED TO COME IN-- I'LL COME OUT!
WHAM
DOWN!

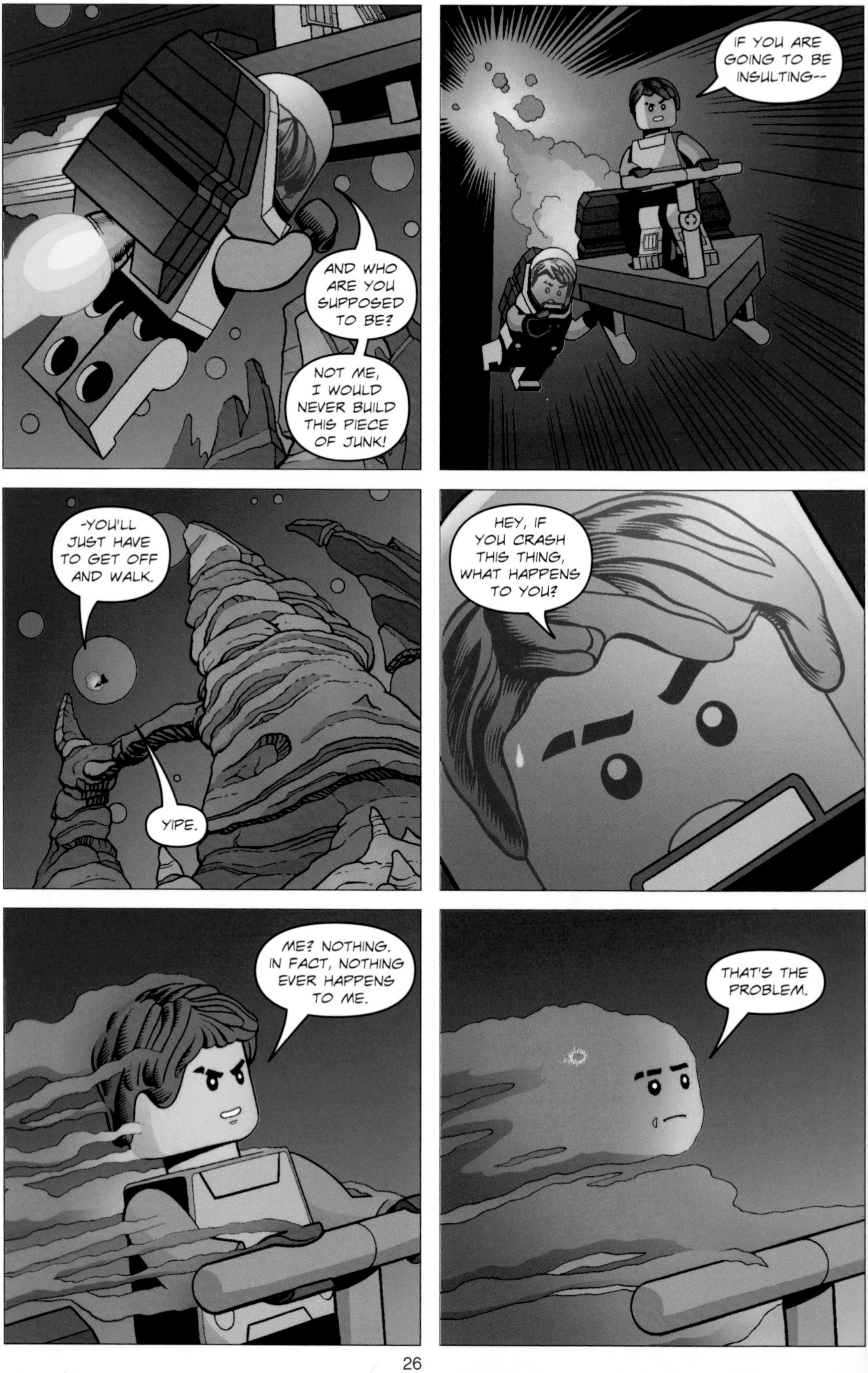
AND WHO ARE YOU SUPPOSED TO BE?
NOT ME, I WOULD NEVER BUILD THIS PIECE OF JUNK!
IF YOU ARE GOING TO BE INSULTING--
-YOU'LL JUST HAVE TO GET OFF AND WALK.
YIPE.
HEY, IF YOU CRASH THIS THING, WHAT HAPPENS TO YOU?
ME? NOTHING. IN FACT, NOTHING EVER HAPPENS TO ME.
THAT'S THE PROBLEM.

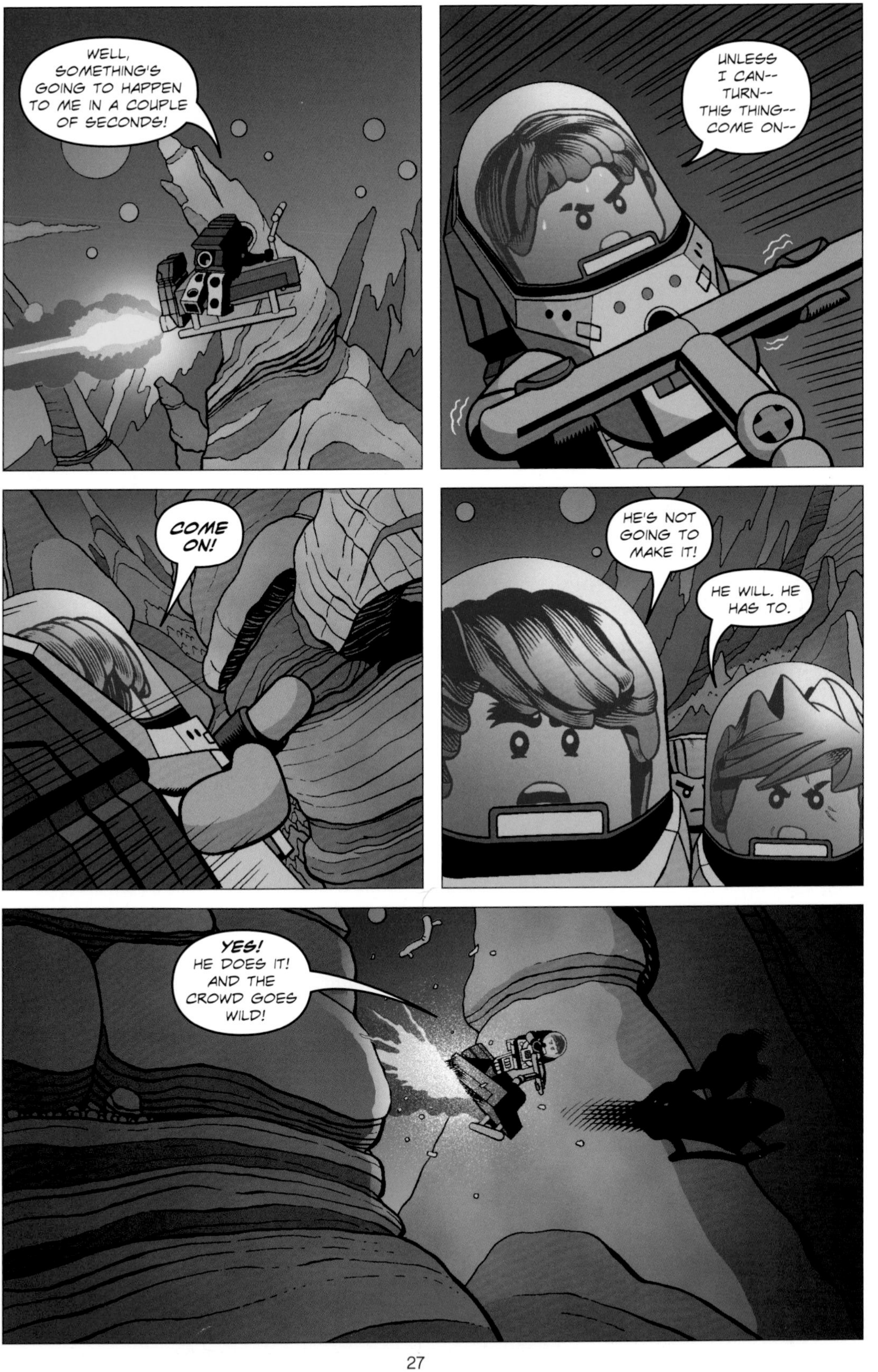
WELL, SOMETHING'S GOING TO HAPPEN TO ME IN A COUPLE OF SECONDS!
UNLESS I CAN-- TURN-- THIS THING-- COME ON--
COME ON!
HE'S NOT GOING TO MAKE IT!
HE WILL. HE HAS TO.
YES! HE DOES IT! AND THE CROWD GOES WILD!

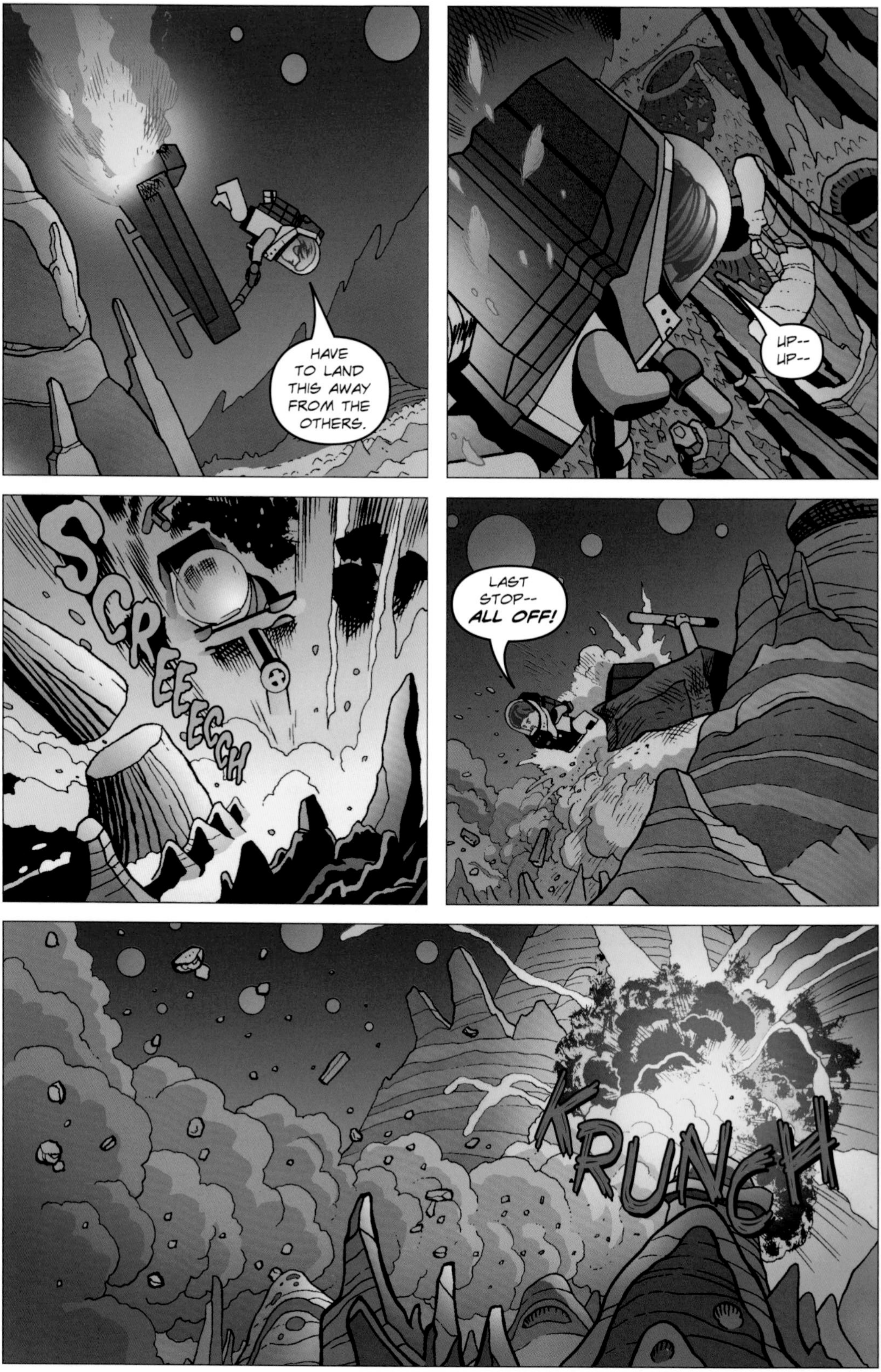
HAVE TO LAND THIS AWAY FROM THE OTHERS.
UP-- UP--
SCREEEECCH
LAST STOP-- **ALL OFF!**
KRUNCH

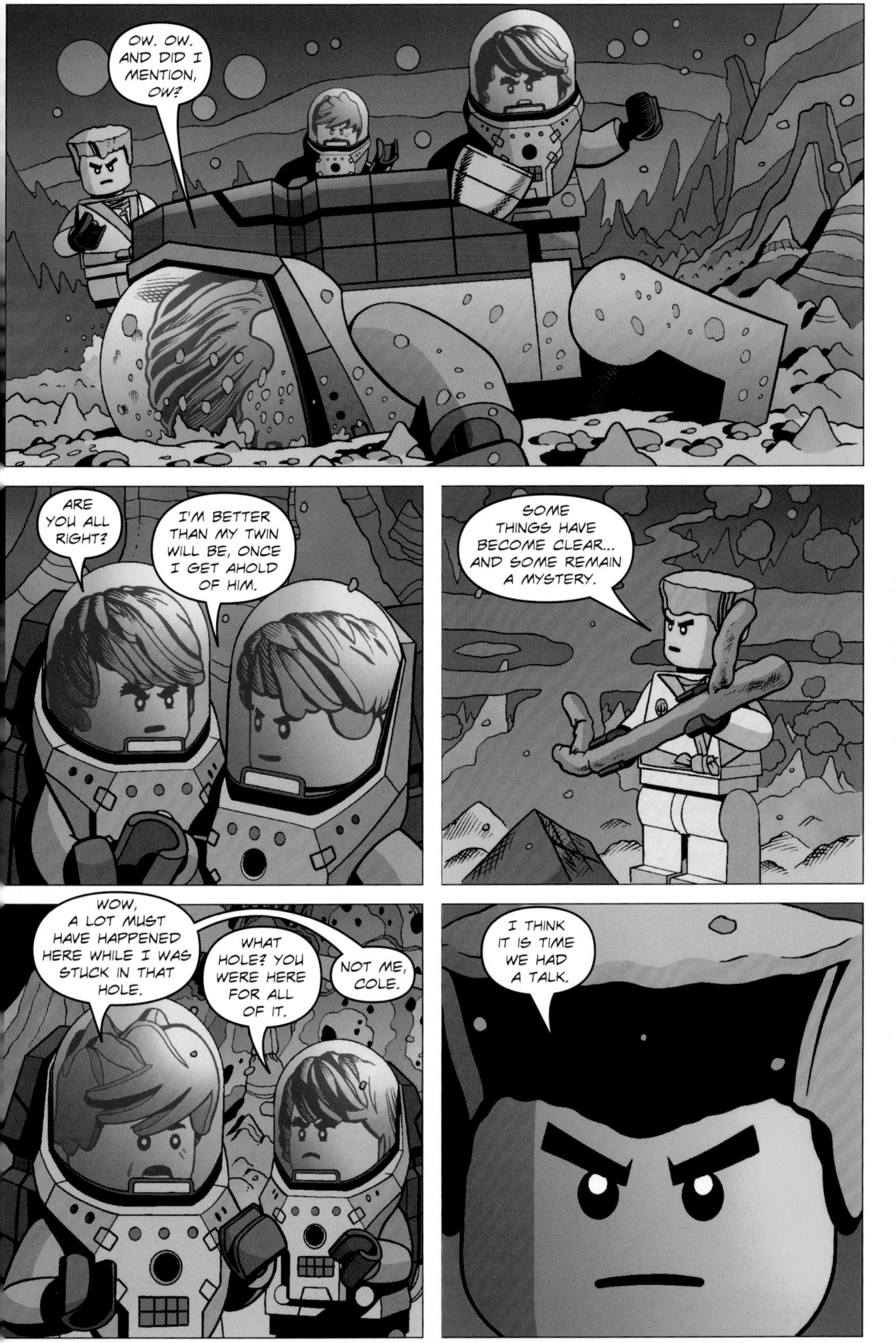
OW. OW. AND DID I MENTION, OW?
ARE YOU ALL RIGHT?
I'M BETTER THAN MY TWIN WILL BE, ONCE I GET AHOLD OF HIM.
SOME THINGS HAVE BECOME CLEAR... AND SOME REMAIN A MYSTERY.
WOW, A LOT MUST HAVE HAPPENED HERE WHILE I WAS STUCK IN THAT HOLE.
WHAT HOLE? YOU WERE HERE FOR ALL OF IT.
NOT ME, COLE.
I THINK IT IS TIME WE HAD A TALK.

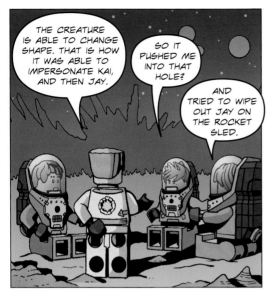

THE CREATURE IS ABLE TO CHANGE SHAPE. THAT IS HOW IT WAS ABLE TO IMPERSONATE KAI, AND THEN JAY.

SO IT PUSHED ME INTO THAT HOLE?

AND TRIED TO WIPE OUT JAY ON THE ROCKET SLED.

MAYBE, MAYBE NOT.

THERE MIGHT HAVE BEEN ENOUGH OF THE REAL JAY IN IT THAT IT KNEW HE COULD ESCAPE.

IT KNEW? I DIDN'T KNOW!

ONE THING WE CAN BE SURE OF:

IT TRIED TO SABOTAGE THE ROCKET.

IT WANTS TO KEEP US HERE.

FROM NOW ON, NONE OF US SHOULD BE ALONE AT ANY TIME.

WOW, ARE WE GOING TO GET TIRED OF EACH OTHER...

HEY, NOBODY COULD EVER GET TIRED OF ME.

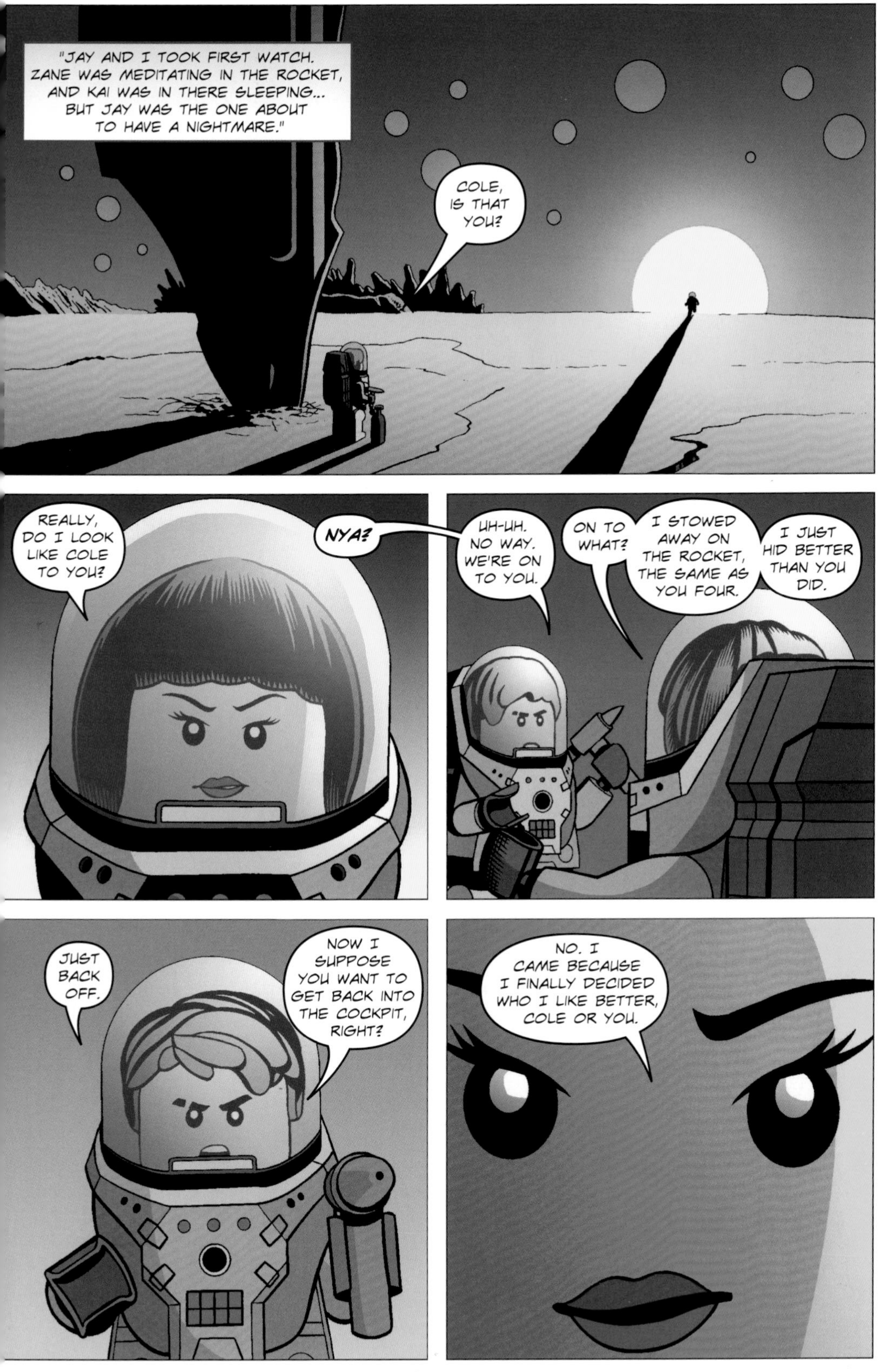
"JAY AND I TOOK FIRST WATCH. ZANE WAS MEDITATING IN THE ROCKET, AND KAI WAS IN THERE SLEEPING... BUT JAY WAS THE ONE ABOUT TO HAVE A NIGHTMARE."
COLE, IS THAT YOU?
REALLY, DO I LOOK LIKE COLE TO YOU?
NYA?
UH-UH. NO WAY. WE'RE ON TO YOU.
ON TO WHAT?
I STOWED AWAY ON THE ROCKET, THE SAME AS YOU FOUR.
I JUST HID BETTER THAN YOU DID.
JUST BACK OFF.
NOW I SUPPOSE YOU WANT TO GET BACK INTO THE COCKPIT, RIGHT?
NO. I CAME BECAUSE I FINALLY DECIDED WHO I LIKE BETTER, COLE OR YOU.

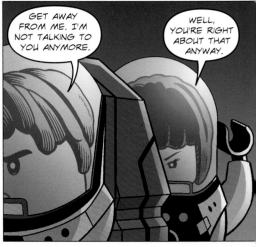

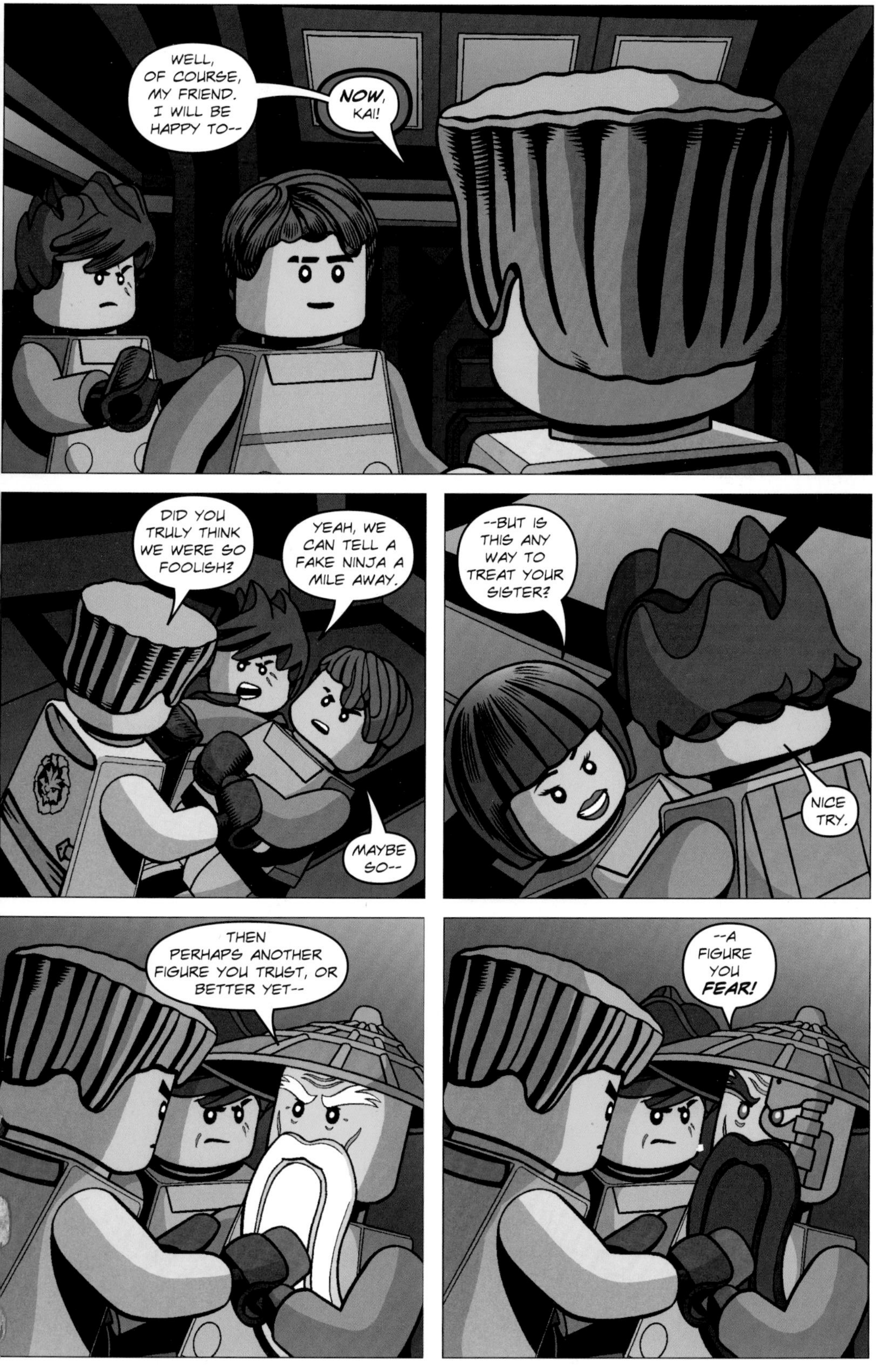
WELL, OF COURSE, MY FRIEND. I WILL BE HAPPY TO--
NOW, KAI!
DID YOU TRULY THINK WE WERE SO FOOLISH?
YEAH, WE CAN TELL A FAKE NINJA A MILE AWAY.
MAYBE SO--
--BUT IS THIS ANY WAY TO TREAT YOUR SISTER?
NICE TRY.
THEN PERHAPS ANOTHER FIGURE YOU TRUST, OR BETTER YET--
--A FIGURE YOU **FEAR!**

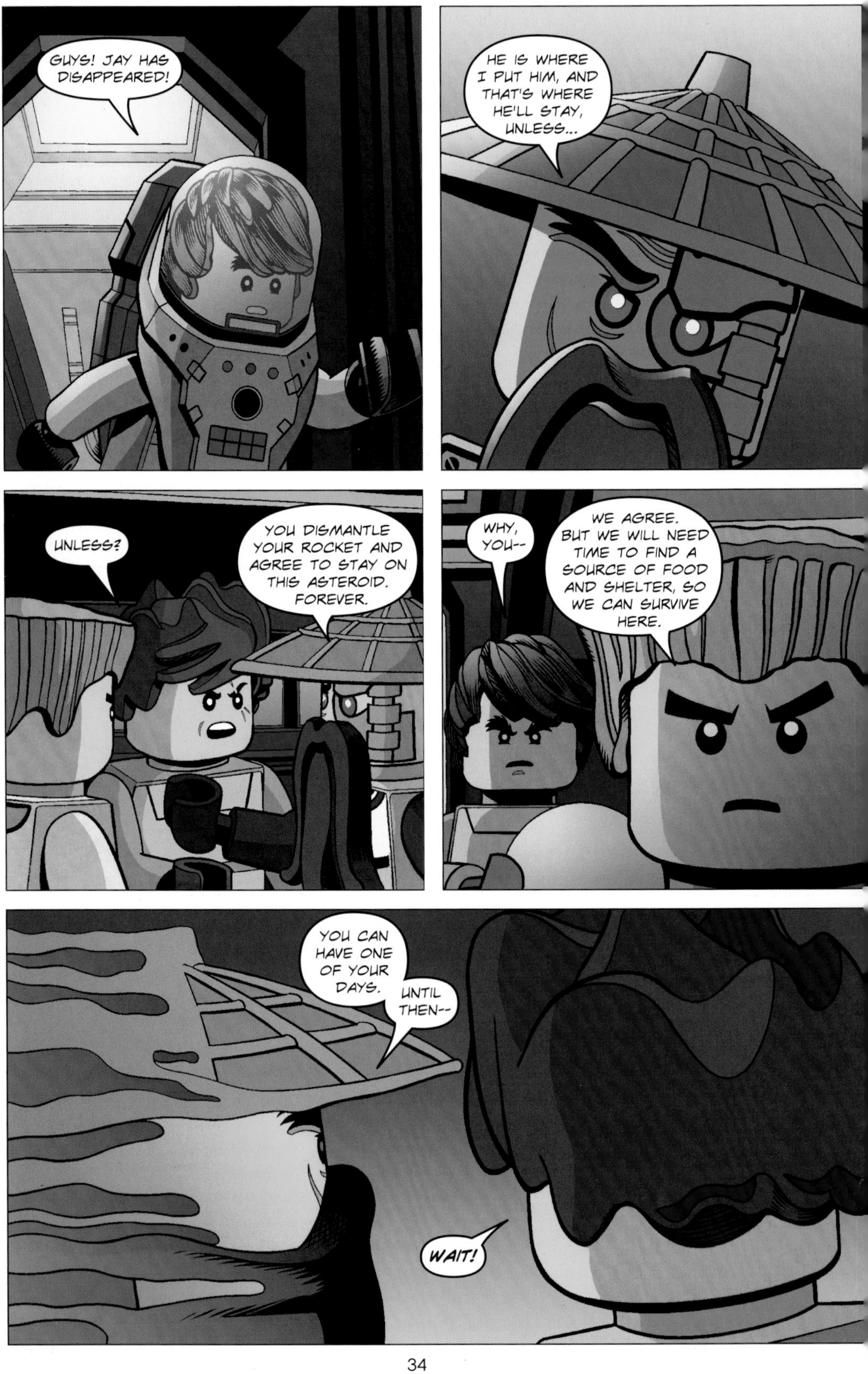
GUYS! JAY HAS DISAPPEARED!
HE IS WHERE I PUT HIM, AND THAT'S WHERE HE'LL STAY, UNLESS...
UNLESS?
YOU DISMANTLE YOUR ROCKET AND AGREE TO STAY ON THIS ASTEROID. FOREVER.
WHY, YOU--
WE AGREE. BUT WE WILL NEED TIME TO FIND A SOURCE OF FOOD AND SHELTER, SO WE CAN SURVIVE HERE.
YOU CAN HAVE ONE OF YOUR DAYS.
UNTIL THEN--
WAIT!

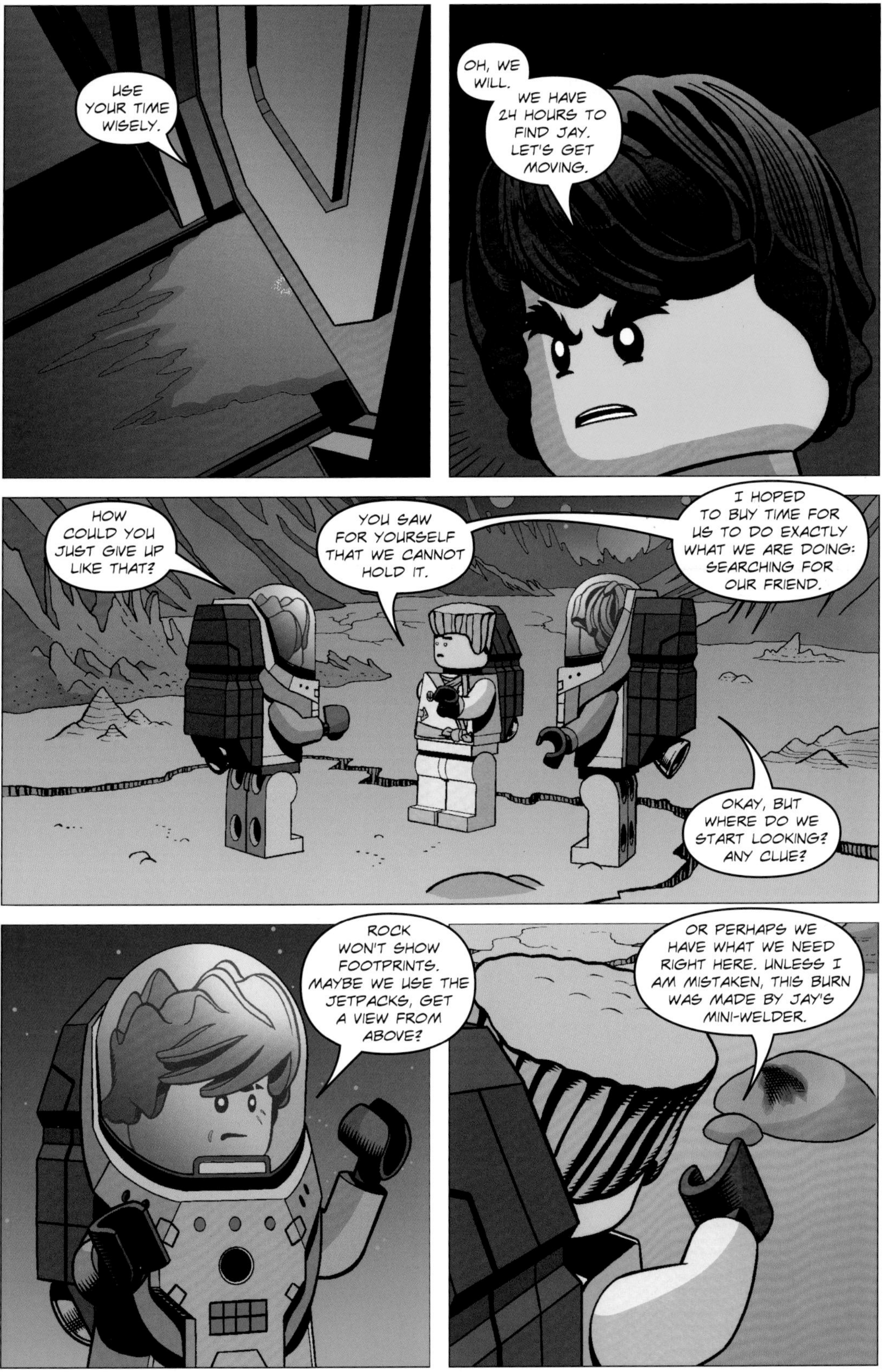
USE YOUR TIME WISELY.
OH, WE WILL.
WE HAVE 24 HOURS TO FIND JAY. LET'S GET MOVING.
HOW COULD YOU JUST GIVE UP LIKE THAT?
YOU SAW FOR YOURSELF THAT WE CANNOT HOLD IT.
I HOPED TO BUY TIME FOR US TO DO EXACTLY WHAT WE ARE DOING: SEARCHING FOR OUR FRIEND.
OKAY, BUT WHERE DO WE START LOOKING? ANY CLUE?
ROCK WON'T SHOW FOOTPRINTS. MAYBE WE USE THE JETPACKS, GET A VIEW FROM ABOVE?
OR PERHAPS WE HAVE WHAT WE NEED RIGHT HERE. UNLESS I AM MISTAKEN, THIS BURN WAS MADE BY JAY'S MINI-WELDER.

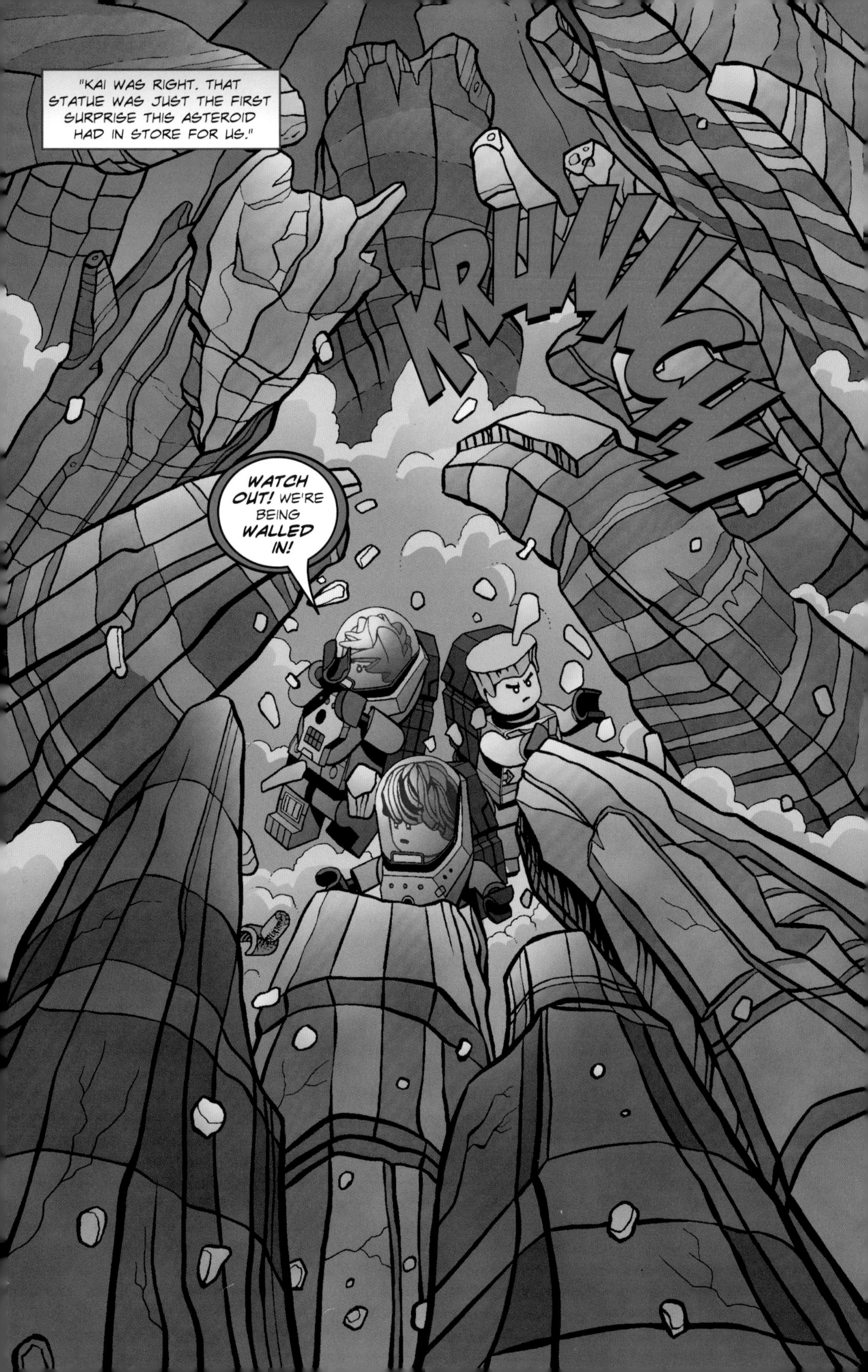
"KAI WAS RIGHT. THAT STATUE WAS JUST THE FIRST SURPRISE THIS ASTEROID HAD IN STORE FOR US."
KRUNNCHH
WATCH OUT! WE'RE BEING WALLED IN!

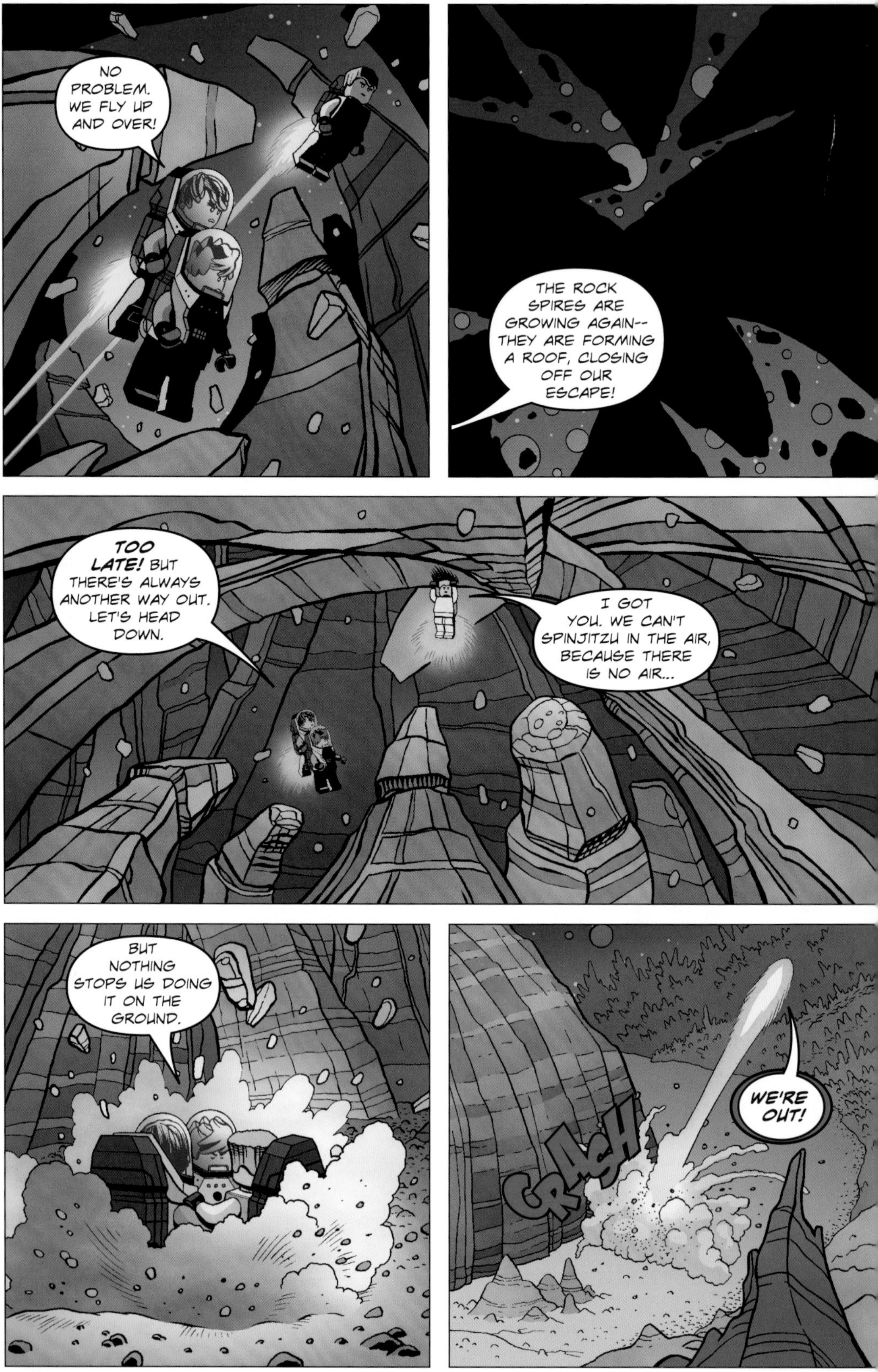
NO PROBLEM. WE FLY UP AND OVER!
THE ROCK SPIRES ARE GROWING AGAIN-- THEY ARE FORMING A ROOF, CLOSING OFF OUR ESCAPE!
TOO LATE! BUT THERE'S ALWAYS ANOTHER WAY OUT. LET'S HEAD DOWN.
I GOT YOU. WE CAN'T SPINJITZU IN THE AIR, BECAUSE THERE IS NO AIR...
BUT NOTHING STOPS US DOING IT ON THE GROUND.
CRASH
WE'RE OUT!

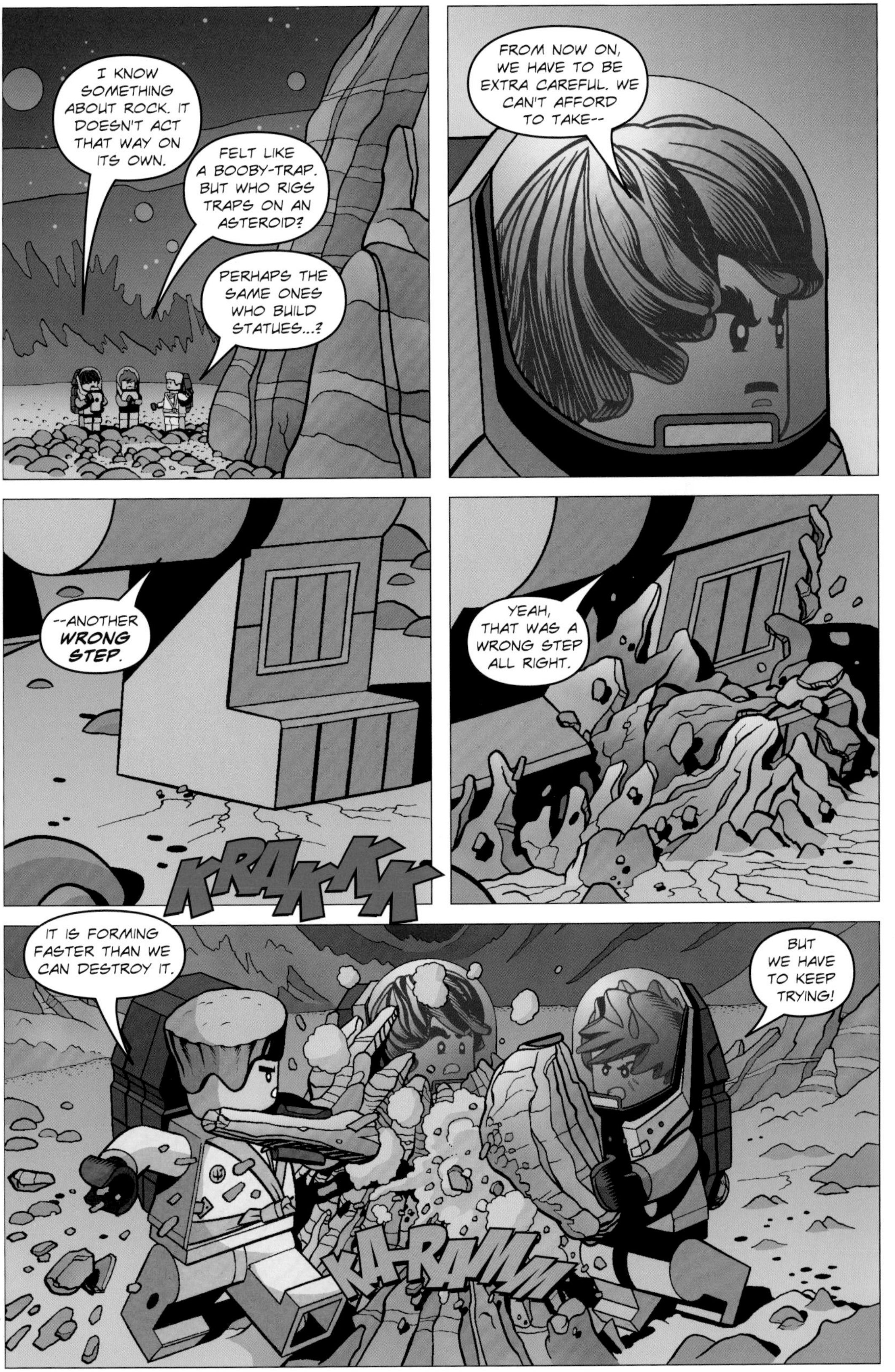
I KNOW SOMETHING ABOUT ROCK. IT DOESN'T ACT THAT WAY ON ITS OWN.
FELT LIKE A BOOBY-TRAP. BUT WHO RIGS TRAPS ON AN ASTEROID?
PERHAPS THE SAME ONES WHO BUILD STATUES...?
FROM NOW ON, WE HAVE TO BE EXTRA CAREFUL. WE CAN'T AFFORD TO TAKE--
--ANOTHER WRONG STEP.
KRAKKK
YEAH, THAT WAS A WRONG STEP ALL RIGHT.
IT IS FORMING FASTER THAN WE CAN DESTROY IT.
BUT WE HAVE TO KEEP TRYING!
KA-RAMM

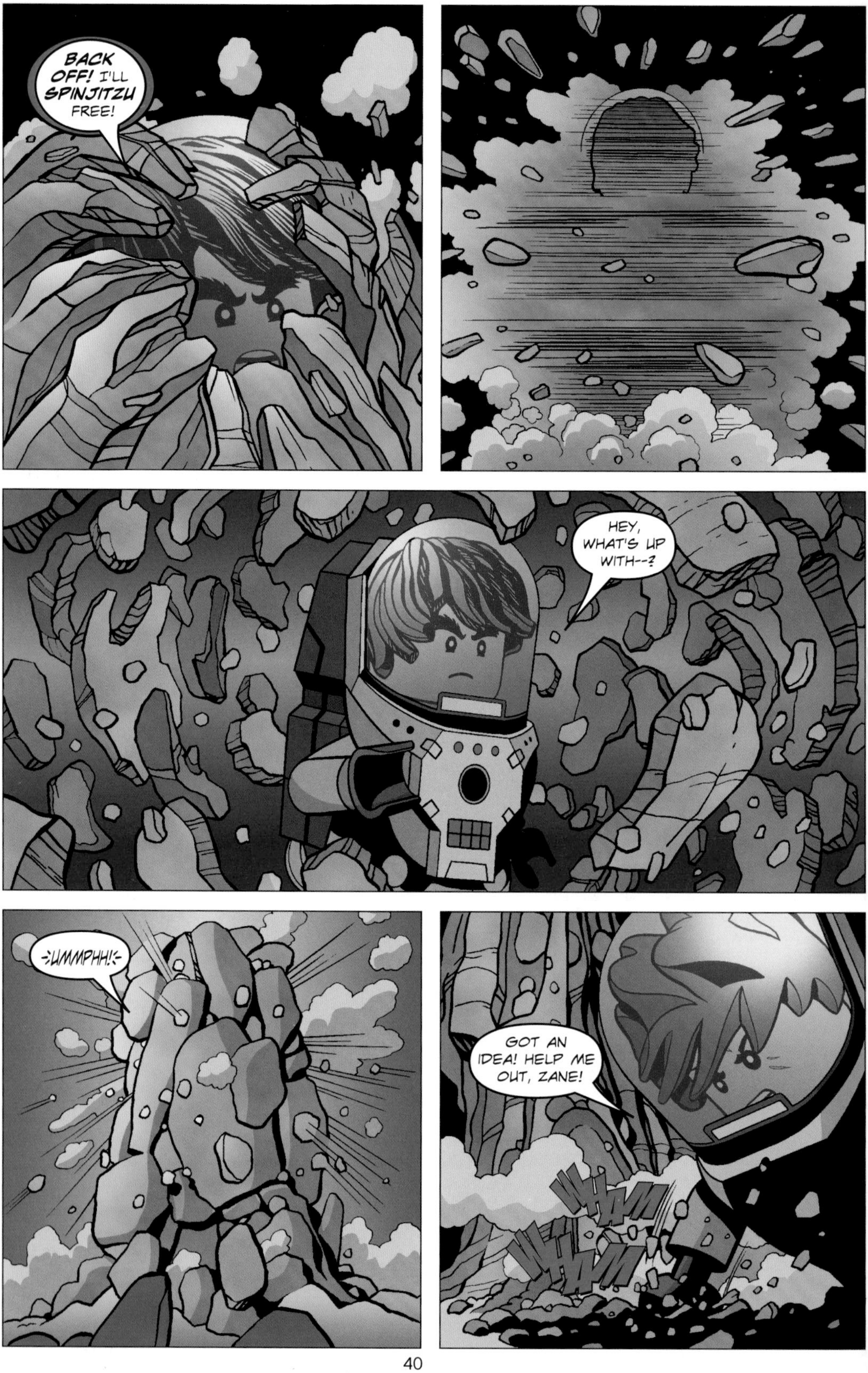
BACK OFF! I'LL SPINJITZU FREE!
HEY, WHAT'S UP WITH--?
-UMMPHH!-
GOT AN IDEA! HELP ME OUT, ZANE!
WHAM
WHAM

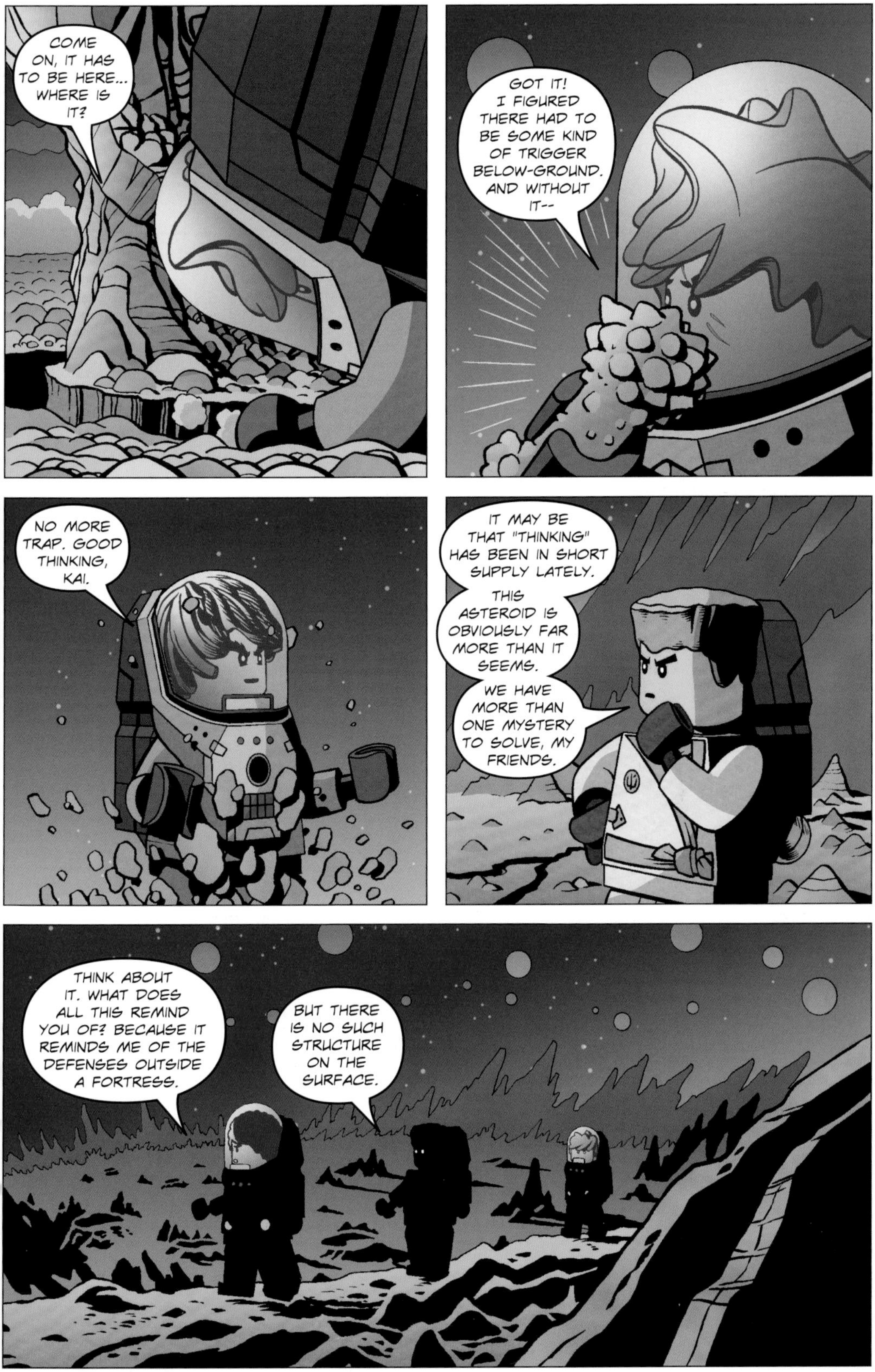
COME ON, IT HAS TO BE HERE... WHERE IS IT?
GOT IT! I FIGURED THERE HAD TO BE SOME KIND OF TRIGGER BELOW-GROUND. AND WITHOUT IT--
NO MORE TRAP. GOOD THINKING, KAI.
IT MAY BE THAT "THINKING" HAS BEEN IN SHORT SUPPLY LATELY.
THIS ASTEROID IS OBVIOUSLY FAR MORE THAN IT SEEMS.
WE HAVE MORE THAN ONE MYSTERY TO SOLVE, MY FRIENDS.
THINK ABOUT IT. WHAT DOES ALL THIS REMIND YOU OF? BECAUSE IT REMINDS ME OF THE DEFENSES OUTSIDE A FORTRESS.
BUT THERE IS NO SUCH STRUCTURE ON THE SURFACE.

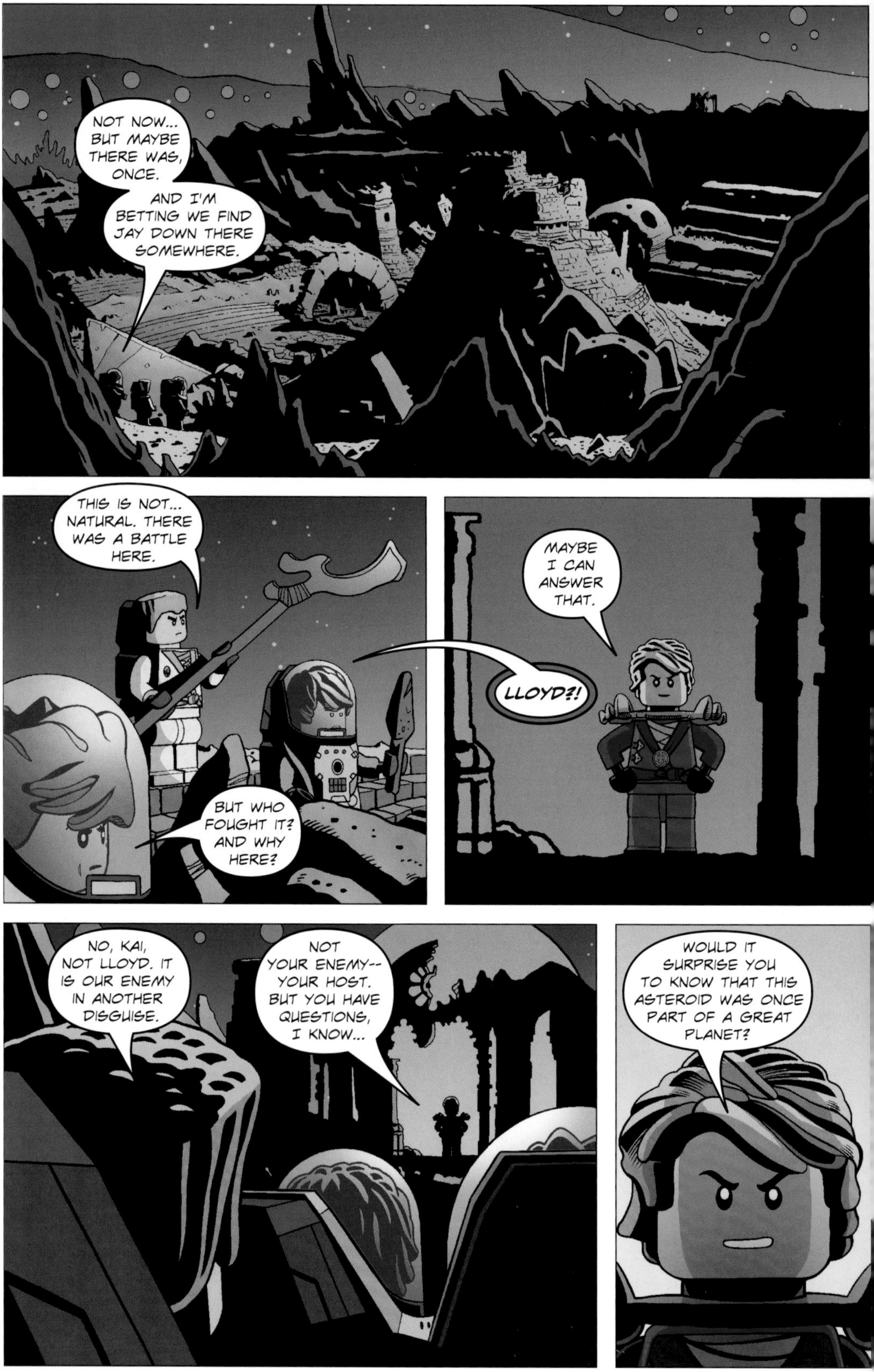

NOT NOW... BUT MAYBE THERE WAS, ONCE.
AND I'M BETTING WE FIND JAY DOWN THERE SOMEWHERE.
THIS IS NOT... NATURAL. THERE WAS A BATTLE HERE.
BUT WHO FOUGHT IT? AND WHY HERE?
MAYBE I CAN ANSWER THAT.
LLOYD?!
NO, KAI, NOT LLOYD. IT IS OUR ENEMY IN ANOTHER DISGUISE.
NOT YOUR ENEMY-- YOUR HOST. BUT YOU HAVE QUESTIONS, I KNOW...
WOULD IT SURPRISE YOU TO KNOW THAT THIS ASTEROID WAS ONCE PART OF A GREAT PLANET?

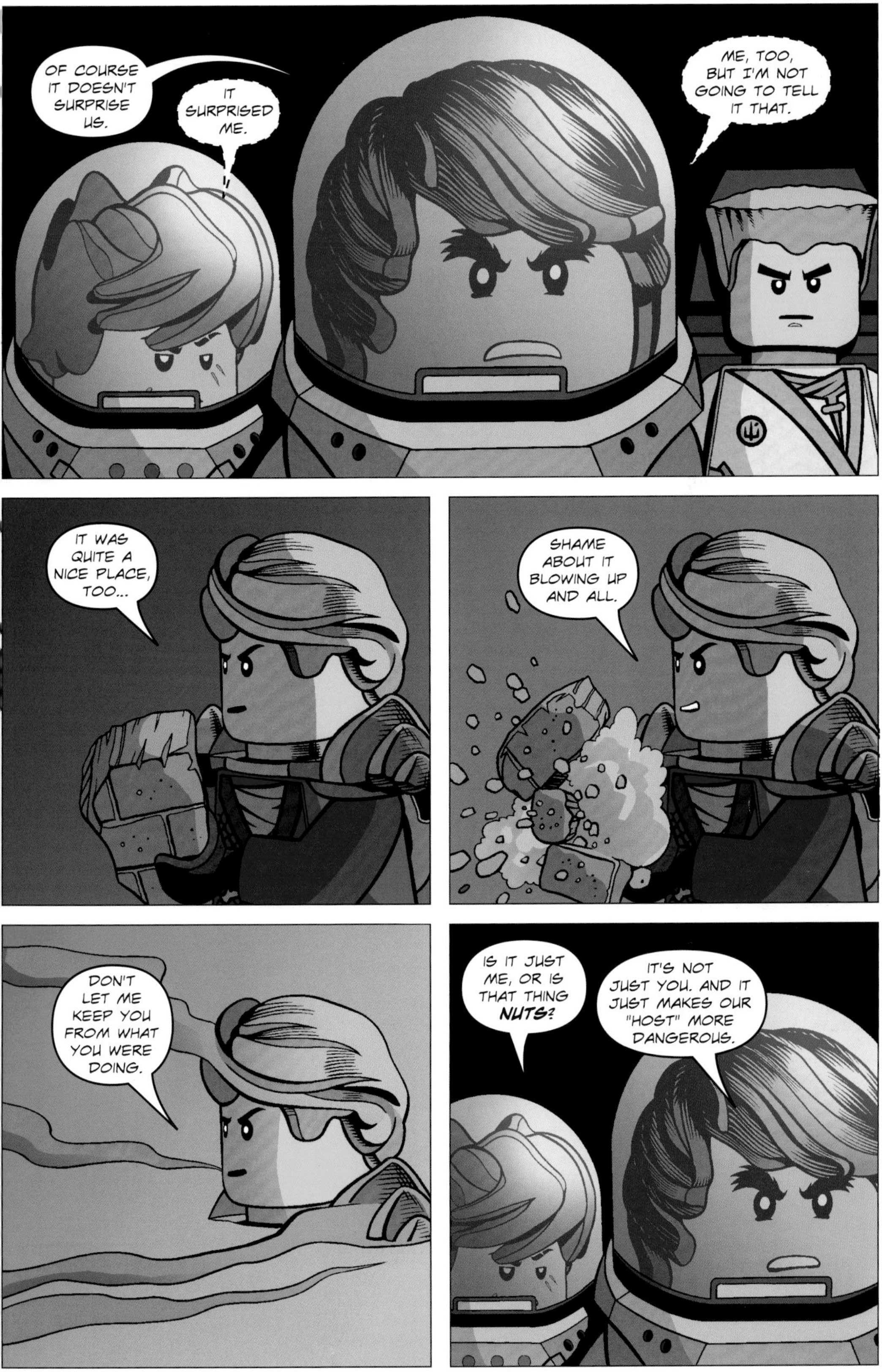
OF COURSE IT DOESN'T SURPRISE US.
IT SURPRISED ME.
ME, TOO, BUT I'M NOT GOING TO TELL IT THAT.
IT WAS QUITE A NICE PLACE, TOO...
SHAME ABOUT IT BLOWING UP AND ALL.
DON'T LET ME KEEP YOU FROM WHAT YOU WERE DOING.
IS IT JUST ME, OR IS THAT THING **NUTS?**
IT'S NOT JUST YOU. AND IT JUST MAKES OUR "HOST" MORE DANGEROUS.

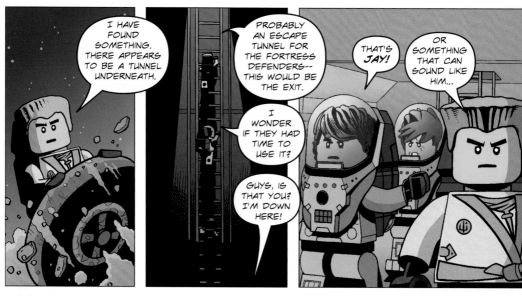

45

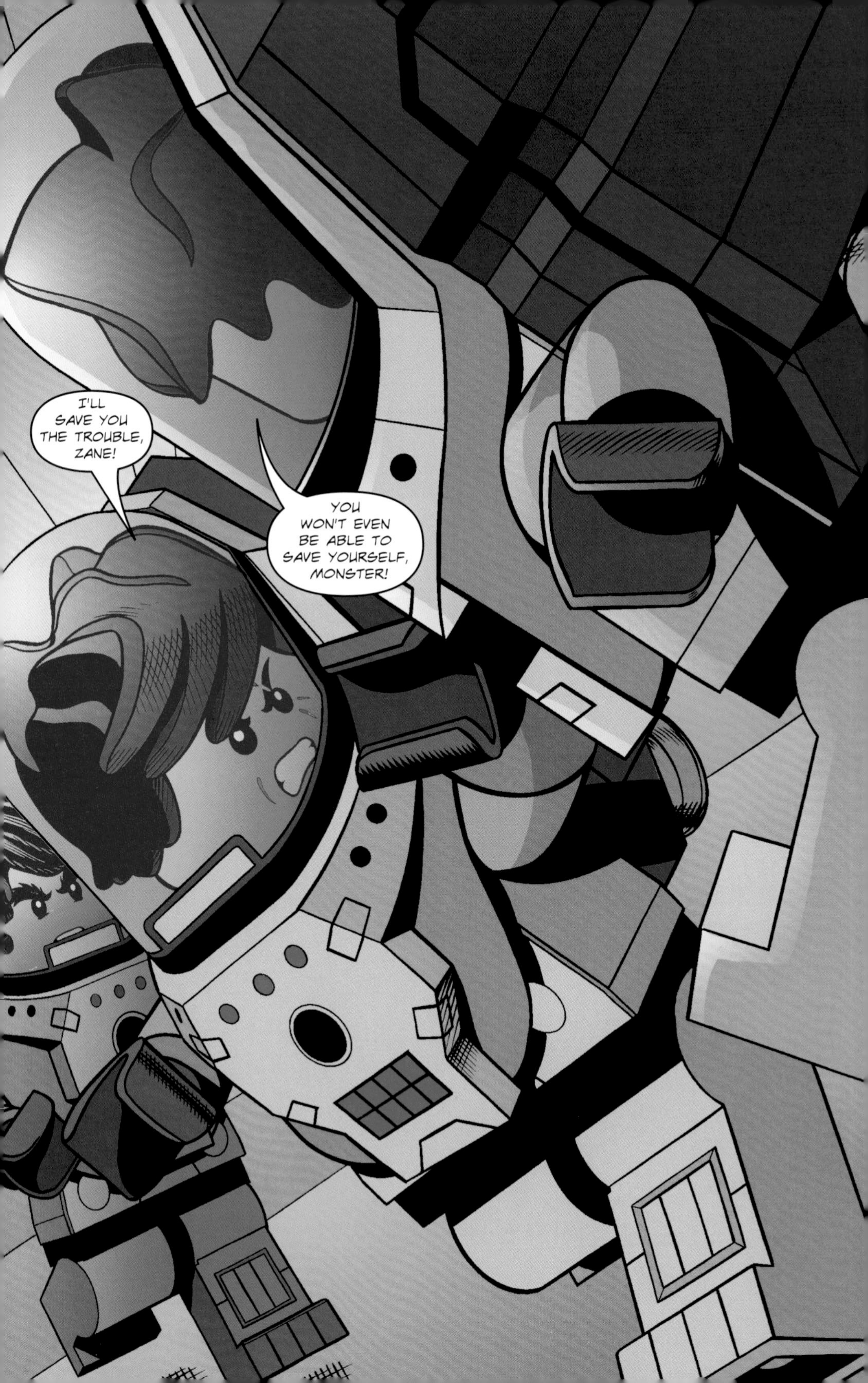
I'LL SAVE YOU THE TROUBLE, ZANE!
YOU WON'T EVEN BE ABLE TO SAVE YOURSELF, MONSTER!

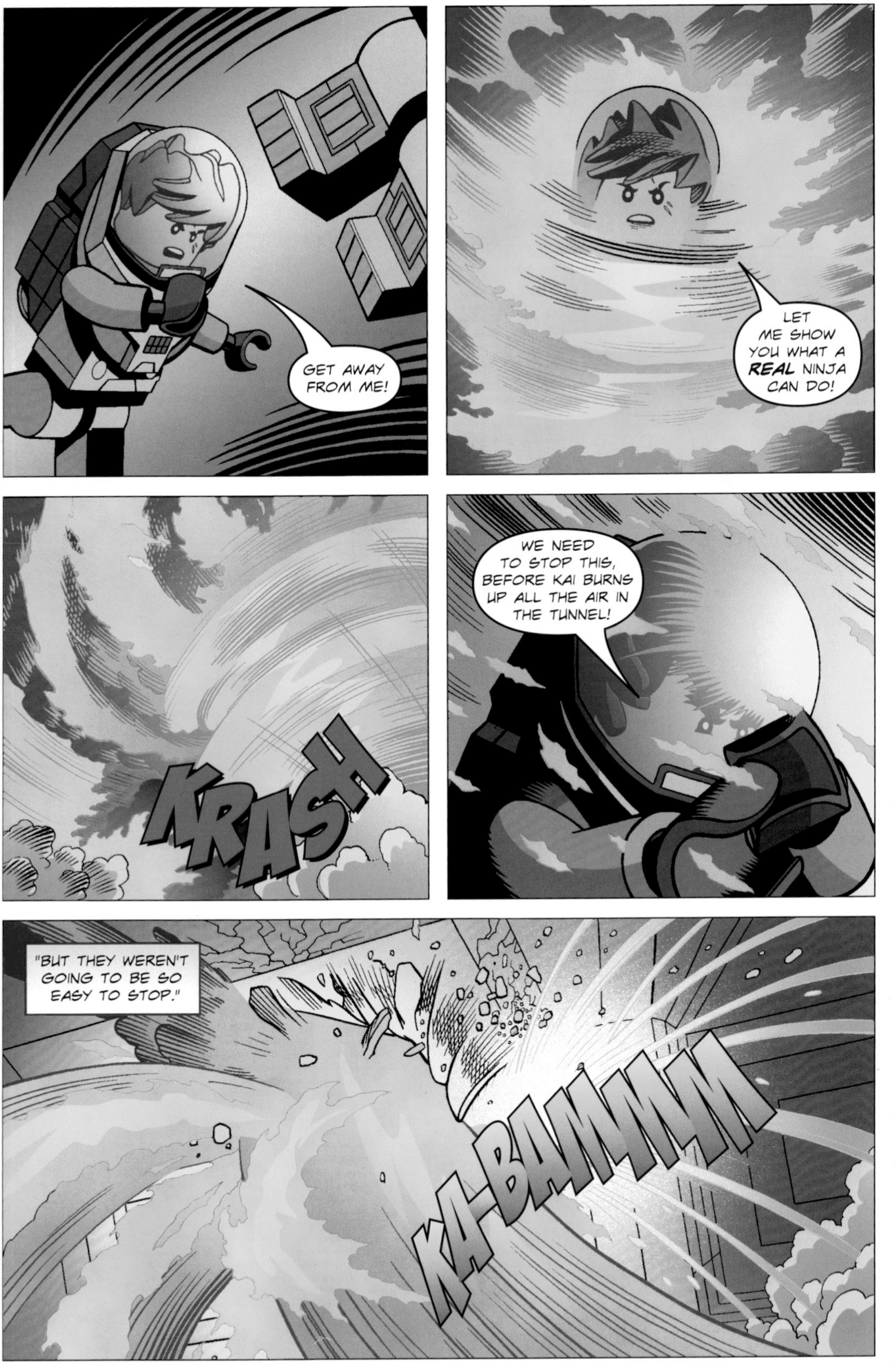
GET AWAY FROM ME!
LET ME SHOW YOU WHAT A **REAL** NINJA CAN DO!
KRASH
WE NEED TO STOP THIS, BEFORE KAI BURNS UP ALL THE AIR IN THE TUNNEL!
"BUT THEY WEREN'T GOING TO BE SO EASY TO STOP."
KA-BAMMMM

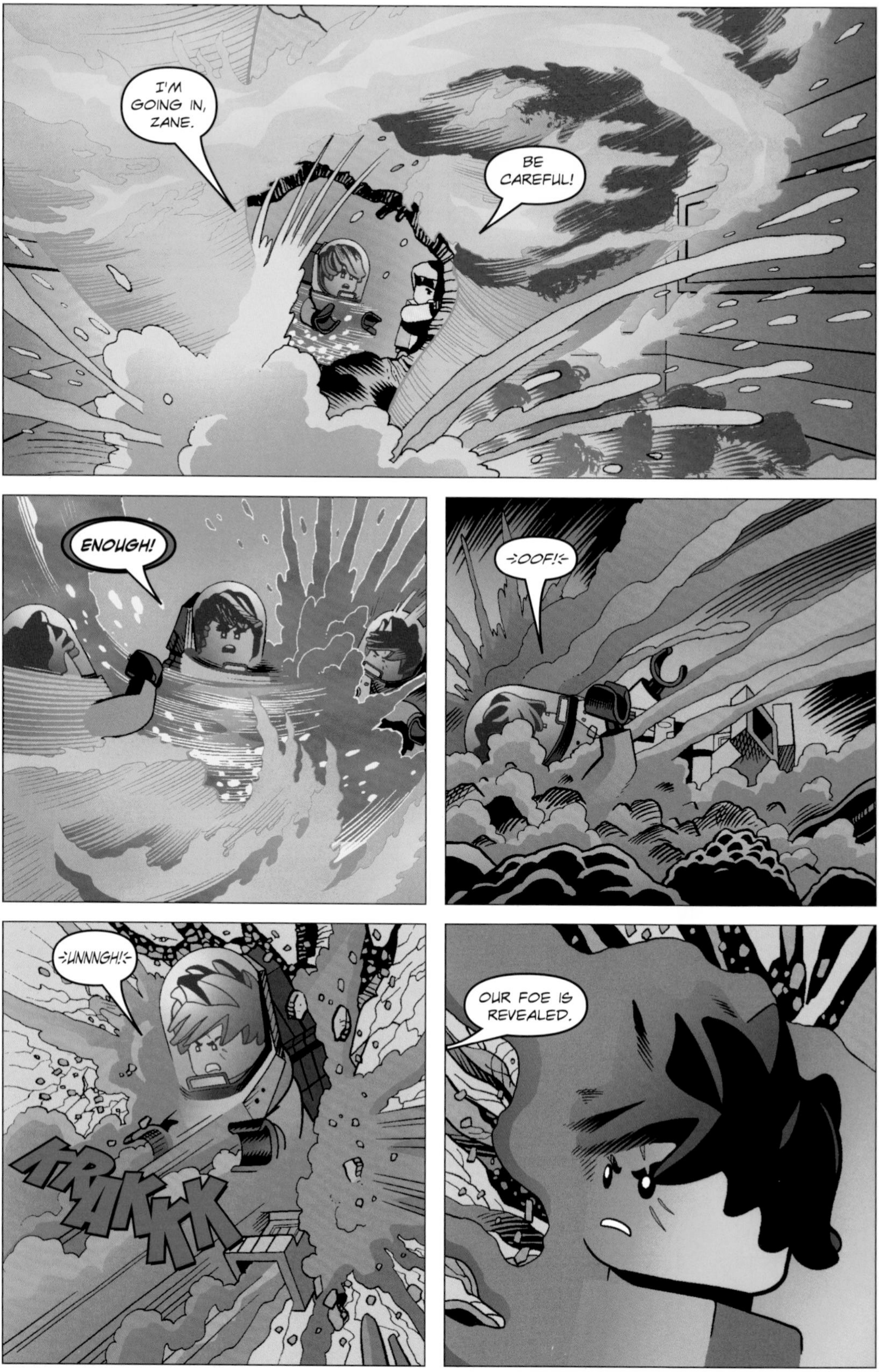
I'M GOING IN, ZANE.
BE CAREFUL!
ENOUGH!
OOF!
UNNNGH!
KRAKKK
OUR FOE IS REVEALED.

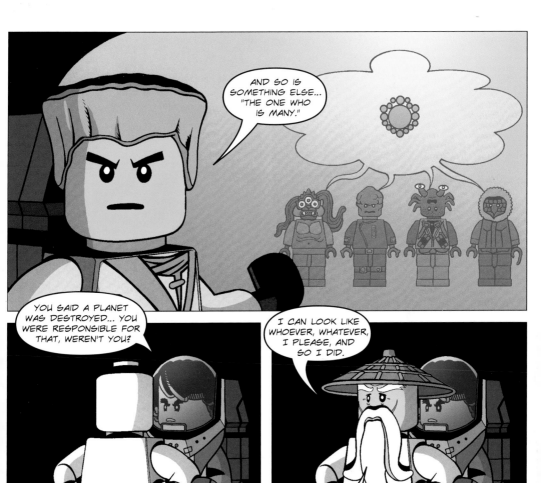

AND SO IS SOMETHING ELSE... "THE ONE WHO IS MANY."

YOU SAID A PLANET WAS DESTROYED... YOU WERE RESPONSIBLE FOR THAT, WEREN'T YOU?

I CAN LOOK LIKE WHOEVER, WHATEVER, I PLEASE, AND SO I DID.

SOON, FRIEND COULD NOT TRUST FRIEND, BECAUSE NO ONE KNEW WHO I MIGHT BE...

AND SUSPICION TURNED TO HATRED, AND HATRED TO BATTLE.

THINGS WENT A BIT TOO FAR...

AND THE WHOLE PLACE WENT TO *PIECES*.

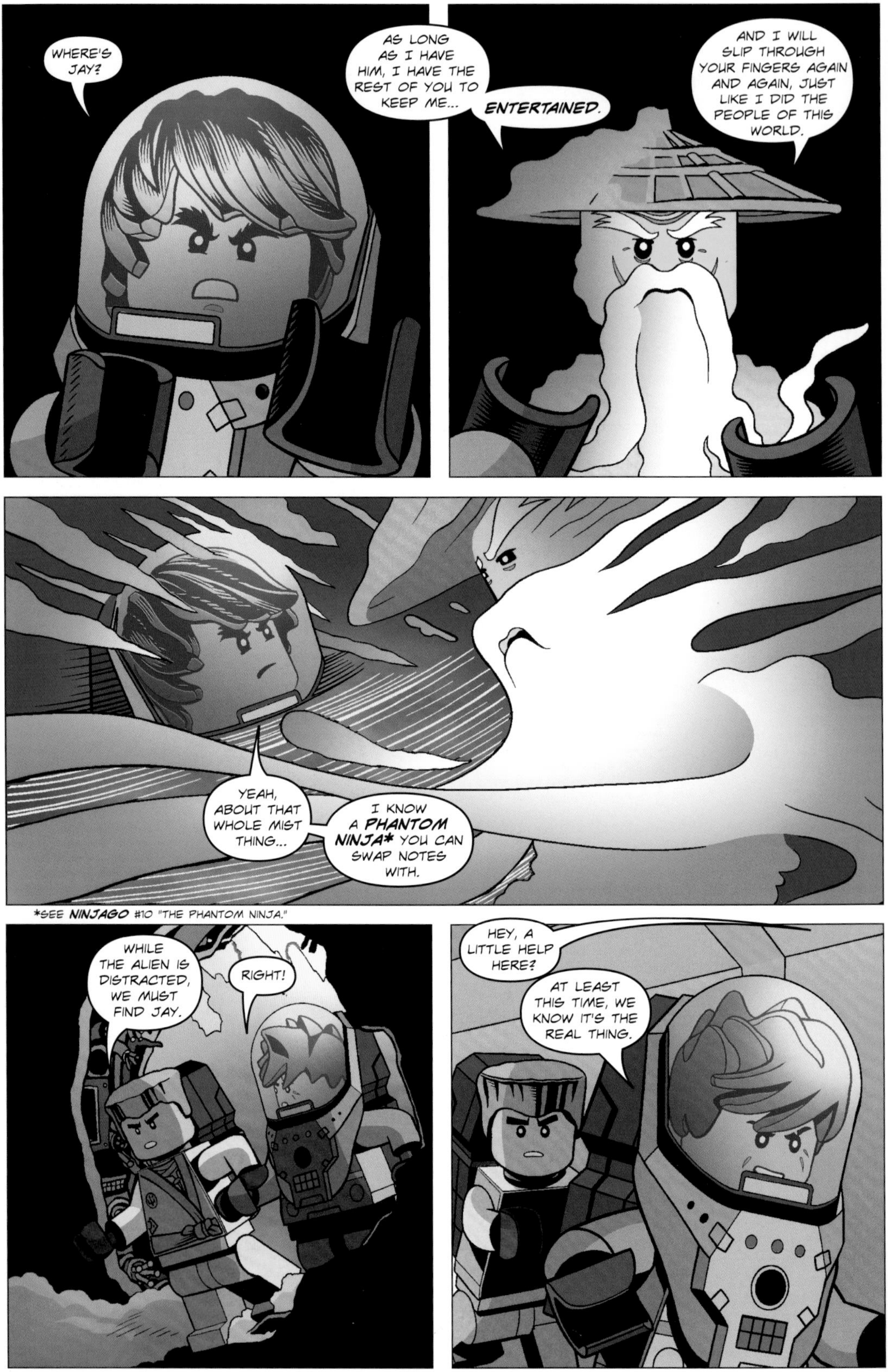
WHERE'S JAY?
AS LONG AS I HAVE HIM, I HAVE THE REST OF YOU TO KEEP ME...
ENTERTAINED.
AND I WILL SLIP THROUGH YOUR FINGERS AGAIN AND AGAIN, JUST LIKE I DID THE PEOPLE OF THIS WORLD.
YEAH, ABOUT THAT WHOLE MIST THING...
I KNOW A PHANTOM NINJA* YOU CAN SWAP NOTES WITH.
*SEE NINJAGO #10 "THE PHANTOM NINJA."
WHILE THE ALIEN IS DISTRACTED, WE MUST FIND JAY.
RIGHT!
HEY, A LITTLE HELP HERE?
AT LEAST THIS TIME, WE KNOW IT'S THE REAL THING.

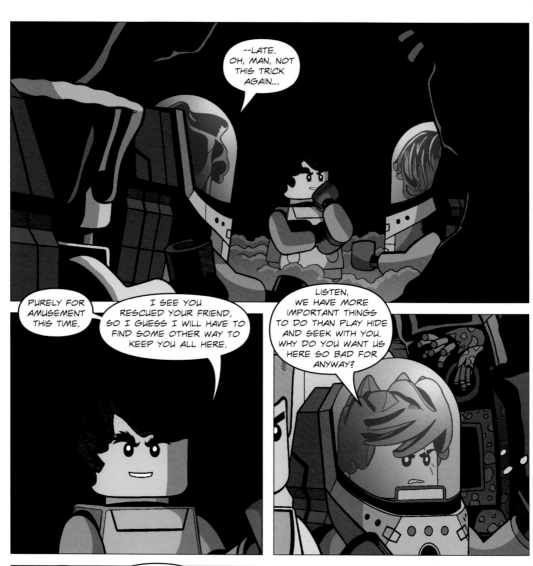

--LATE.
OH, MAN, NOT
THIS TRICK
AGAIN...

PURELY FOR
AMUSEMENT
THIS TIME.

I SEE YOU
RESCUED YOUR FRIEND,
SO I GUESS I WILL HAVE TO
FIND SOME OTHER WAY TO
KEEP YOU ALL HERE.

LISTEN,
WE HAVE MORE
IMPORTANT THINGS
TO DO THAN PLAY HIDE
AND SEEK WITH YOU.
WHY DO YOU WANT US
HERE SO BAD FOR
ANYWAY?

WHY, FOR
COMPANY, OF
COURSE.

THERE IS NO
OTHER INTELLIGENT
LIFE HERE. I NEED
SOMETHING TO
COPY...

SOMETHING
TO TOY WITH...
OR THE DAYS
ARE JUST TOO
LONG.

YOU NEED
ENTERTAINMENT?
THEN A WAGER,
CREATURE...

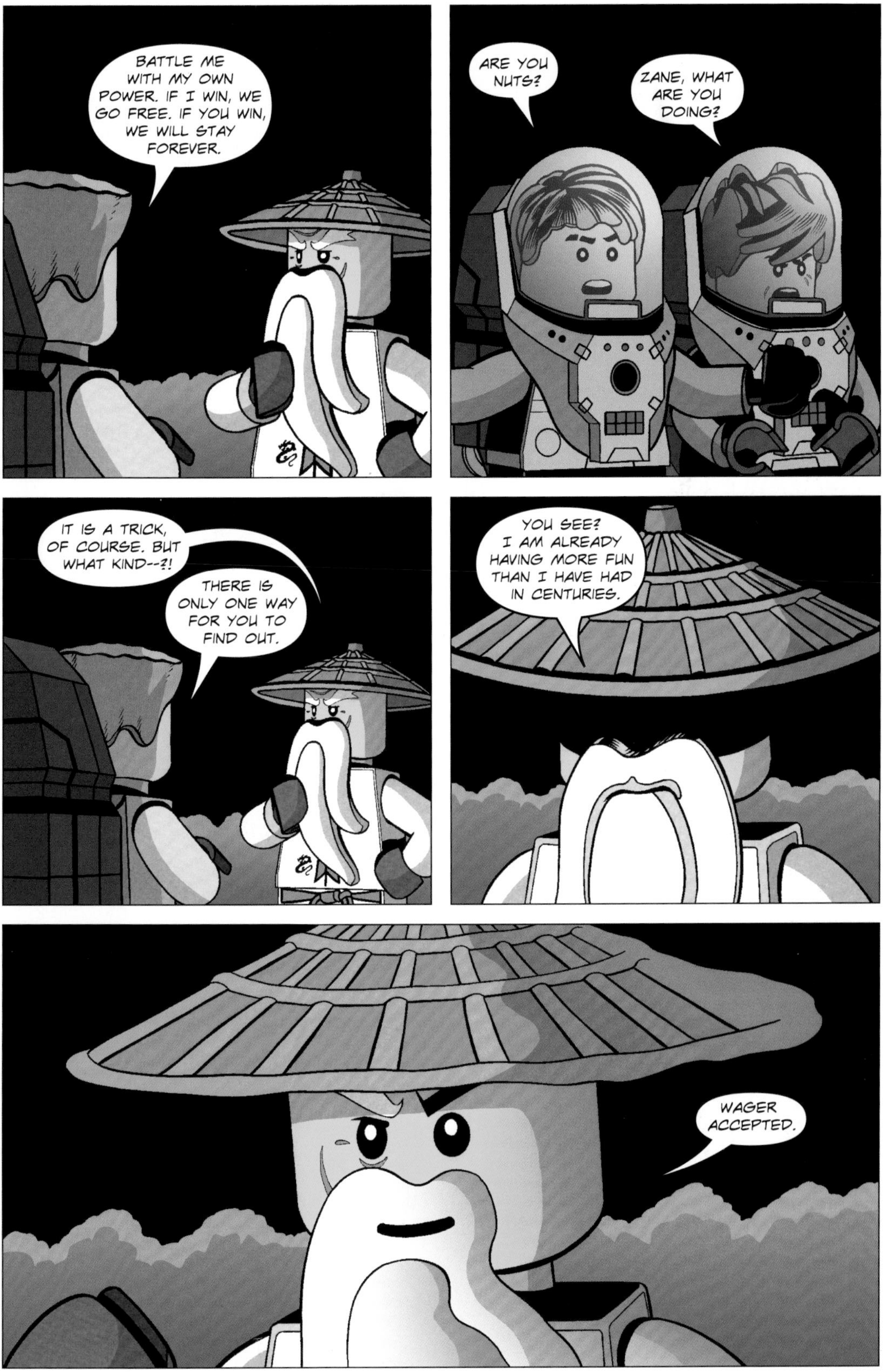
BATTLE ME WITH MY OWN POWER. IF I WIN, WE GO FREE. IF YOU WIN, WE WILL STAY FOREVER.
ARE YOU NUTS?
ZANE, WHAT ARE YOU DOING?
IT IS A TRICK, OF COURSE. BUT WHAT KIND--?!
THERE IS ONLY ONE WAY FOR YOU TO FIND OUT.
YOU SEE? I AM ALREADY HAVING MORE FUN THAN I HAVE HAD IN CENTURIES.
WAGER ACCEPTED.

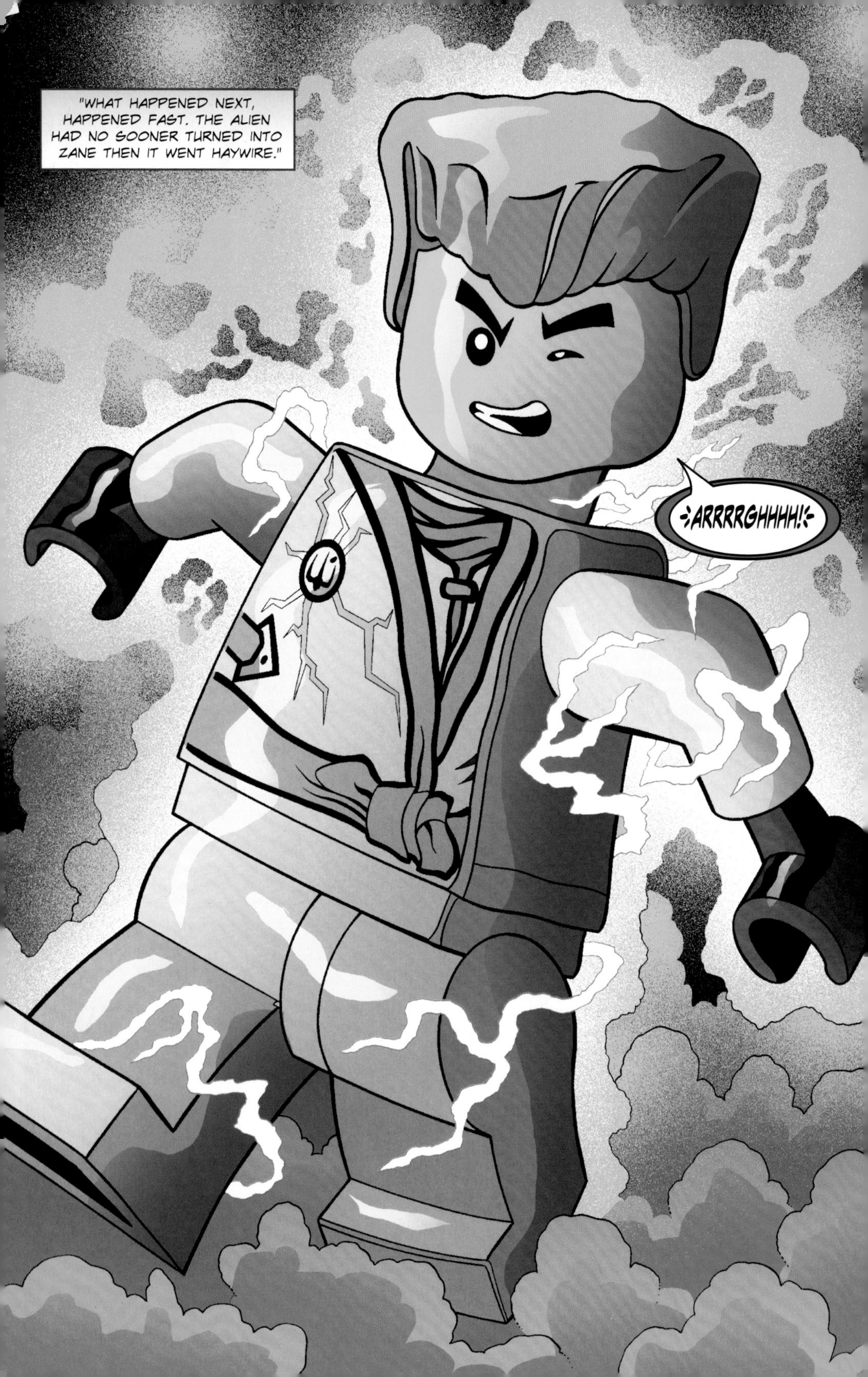
"WHAT HAPPENED NEXT, HAPPENED FAST. THE ALIEN HAD NO SOONER TURNED INTO ZANE THEN IT WENT HAYWIRE."
ARRRRGHHHH!

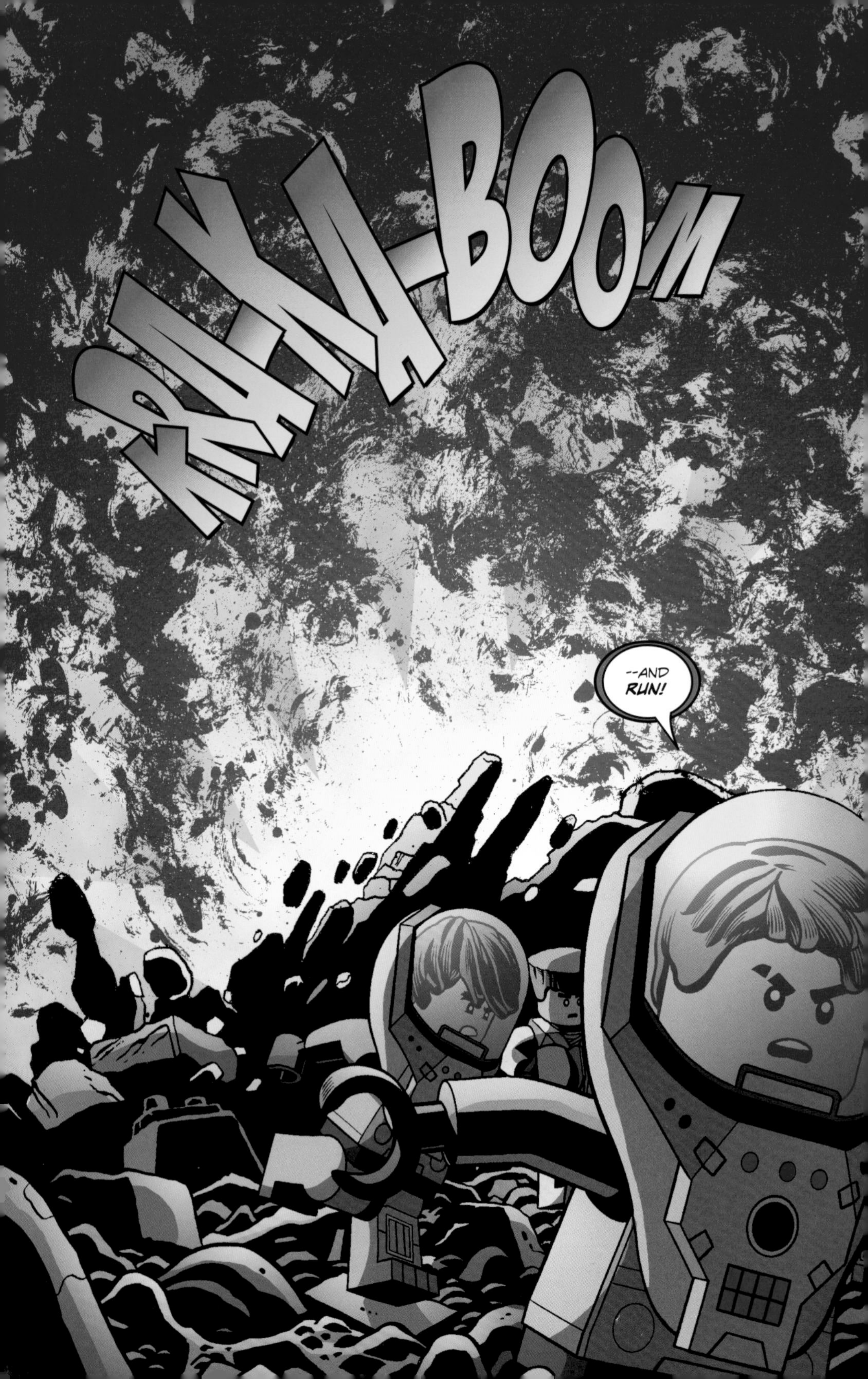
KRAKA-BOOM
--AND RUN!

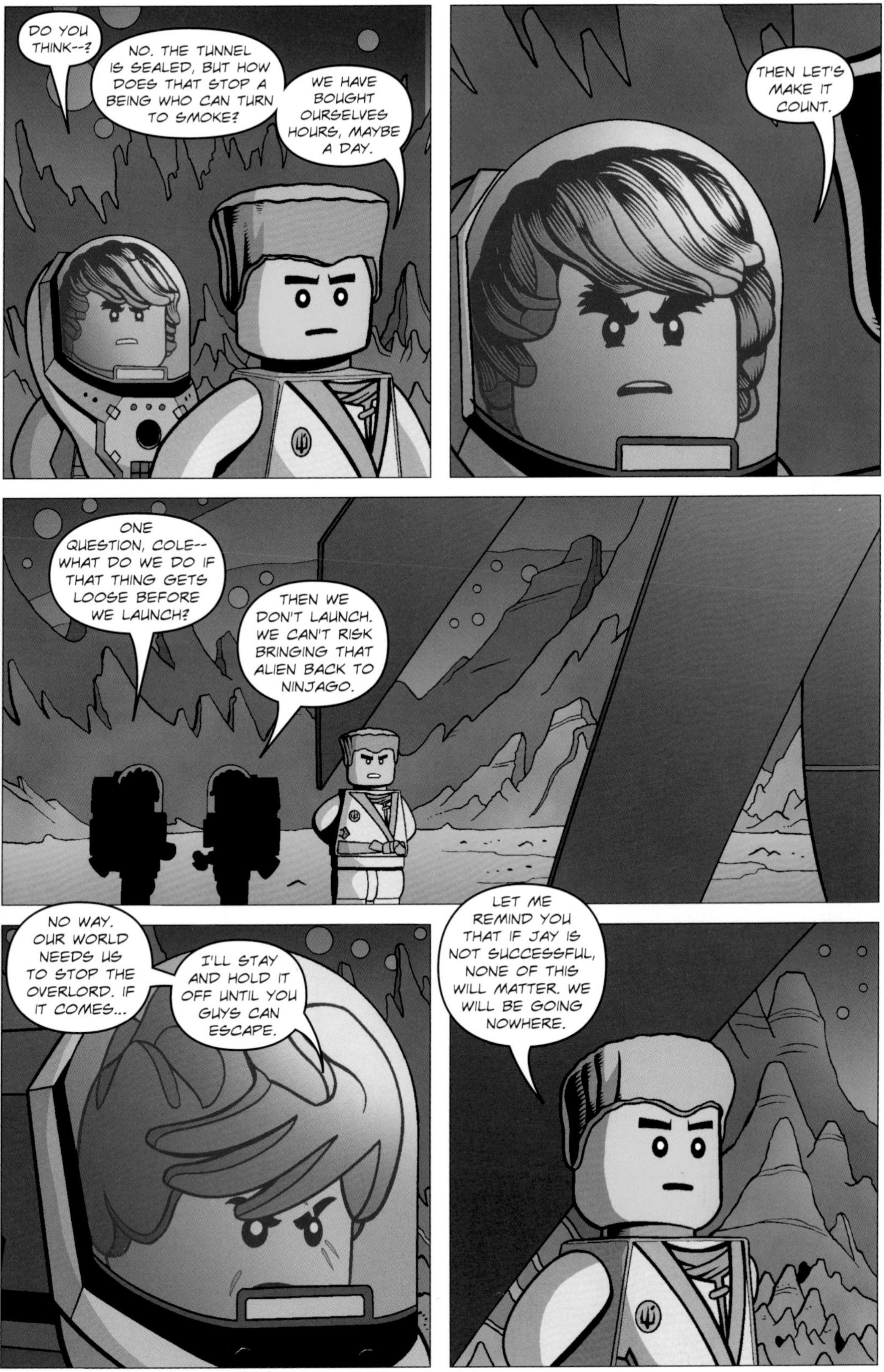
DO YOU THINK--?
NO. THE TUNNEL IS SEALED, BUT HOW DOES THAT STOP A BEING WHO CAN TURN TO SMOKE?
WE HAVE BOUGHT OURSELVES HOURS, MAYBE A DAY.
THEN LET'S MAKE IT COUNT.
ONE QUESTION, COLE-- WHAT DO WE DO IF THAT THING GETS LOOSE BEFORE WE LAUNCH?
THEN WE DON'T LAUNCH. WE CAN'T RISK BRINGING THAT ALIEN BACK TO NINJAGO.
NO WAY. OUR WORLD NEEDS US TO STOP THE OVERLORD. IF IT COMES...
I'LL STAY AND HOLD IT OFF UNTIL YOU GUYS CAN ESCAPE.
LET ME REMIND YOU THAT IF JAY IS NOT SUCCESSFUL, NONE OF THIS WILL MATTER. WE WILL BE GOING NOWHERE.

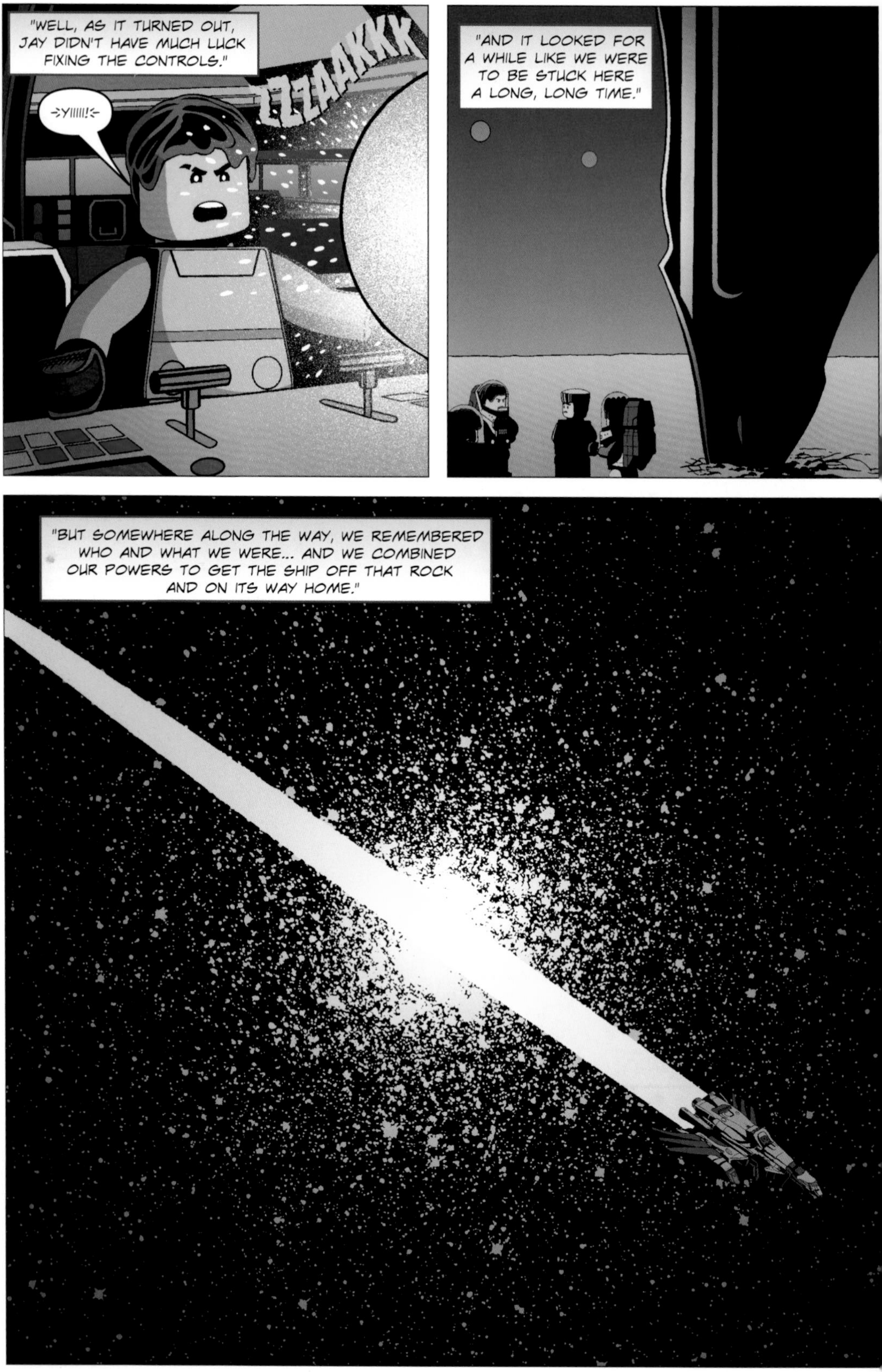
"WELL, AS IT TURNED OUT, JAY DIDN'T HAVE MUCH LUCK FIXING THE CONTROLS."
ZZZAAKKK
YIIIII!
"AND IT LOOKED FOR A WHILE LIKE WE WERE TO BE STUCK HERE A LONG, LONG TIME."
"BUT SOMEWHERE ALONG THE WAY, WE REMEMBERED WHO AND WHAT WE WERE... AND WE COMBINED OUR POWERS TO GET THE SHIP OFF THAT ROCK AND ON ITS WAY HOME."

END

59

LEGO LEGOLAND® PARKS

KIDS GO FREE

with full price adult ticket to LEGOLAND® Parks or LEGOLAND Discovery Centers

Purchase this offer at **LEGOLAND.com/LEGOPapercutzNinjago** now through 12/31/2015.

Offer good for one free one-day child ticket with purchase of a full-price one-day adult ticket to LEGOLAND® California, LEGOLAND Florida or LEGOLAND Discovery Centers. Valid for one complimentary child. Offer cannot be applied to pre-purchased, two day tickets, memberships, online ticket sales or combined with any other discounts or offers. No photocopies or facsimiles will be accepted. Additional restrictions may apply. Prices and hours subject to change without notice. The right of final interpretation resides with LEGOLAND. Not for resale. **Expires 12/31/2015.** **Discount ID 149931**

LEGO LEGOLAND® DISCOVERY CENTER

Atlanta • Boston • Chicago • Dallas/Fort Worth
Kansas City • Toronto • Westchester

Indoor Attraction • LEGO Rides • LEGO MINILAND • 4D Cinema • LEGO Factory Tour • Play Zone • Birthday Room • Shop & Cafe

WATCH OUT FOR PAPERCUTZ™

Welcome to the exciting eleventh LEGO® NINJAGO graphic novel
by Greg Farshtey and Jolyon Yates, from Papercutz, the ever-hopeful
comics company dedicated to publishing great graphic novels for all ages.
I'm Jim Salicrup, the Editor-in-Chief, here with the news we've all been waiting for!

Save this date:

SEPTEMBER 23, 2016

Because that is

when the very first

LEGO NINJAGO movie

will be opening at

a theater near you!

Now, that's awesome!   Thanks,

STAY IN TOUCH!

EMAIL: salicrup@papercutz.com
WEB: papercutz.com
TWITTER: @papercutzgn
FACEBOOK: PAPERCUTZGRAPHICNOVELS
FAN MAIL: Papercutz, 160 Broadway, Suite 700, East Wing,
                New York, NY 10038

Special preview of LEGO LEGEND OF CHIMA #2 "The Right Decision"...

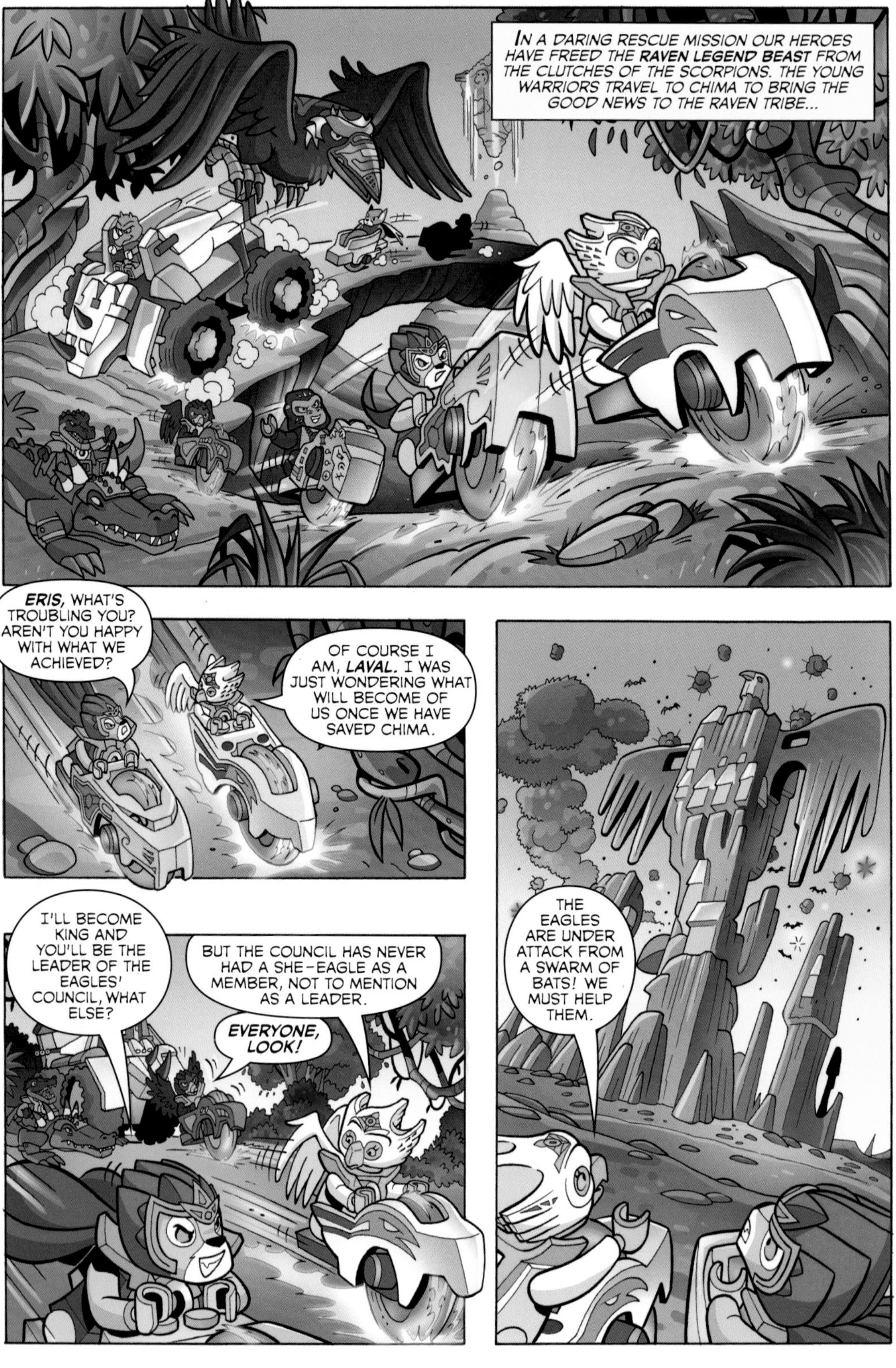
IN A DARING RESCUE MISSION OUR HEROES HAVE FREED THE RAVEN LEGEND BEAST FROM THE CLUTCHES OF THE SCORPIONS. THE YOUNG WARRIORS TRAVEL TO CHIMA TO BRING THE GOOD NEWS TO THE RAVEN TRIBE...
ERIS, WHAT'S TROUBLING YOU? AREN'T YOU HAPPY WITH WHAT WE ACHIEVED?
OF COURSE I AM, LAVAL. I WAS JUST WONDERING WHAT WILL BECOME OF US ONCE WE HAVE SAVED CHIMA.
I'LL BECOME KING AND YOU'LL BE THE LEADER OF THE EAGLES' COUNCIL, WHAT ELSE?
BUT THE COUNCIL HAS NEVER HAD A SHE-EAGLE AS A MEMBER, NOT TO MENTION AS A LEADER.
EVERYONE, LOOK!
THE EAGLES ARE UNDER ATTACK FROM A SWARM OF BATS! WE MUST HELP THEM.

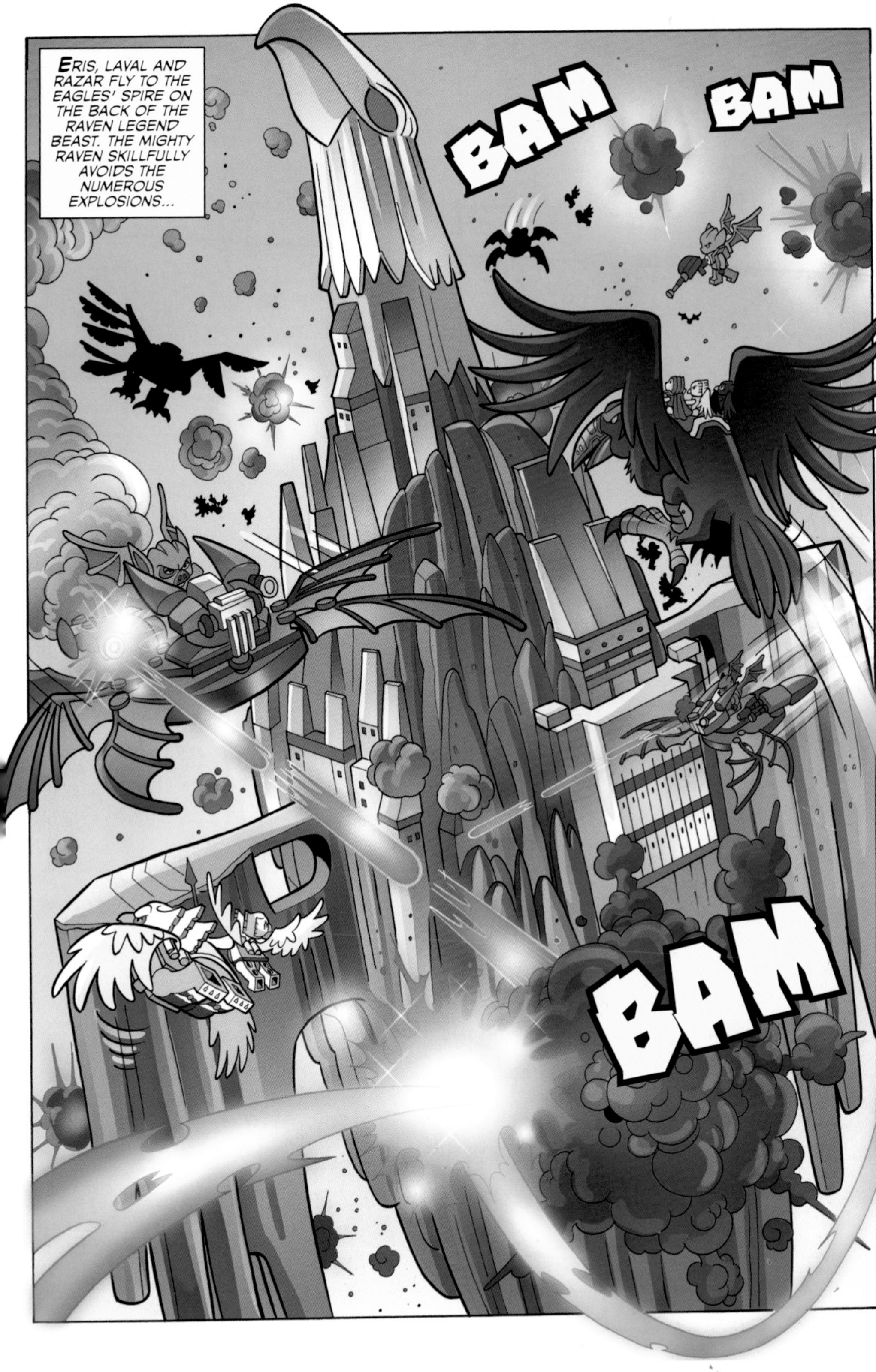
ERIS, LAVAL AND RAZAR FLY TO THE EAGLES' SPIRE ON THE BACK OF THE RAVEN LEGEND BEAST. THE MIGHTY RAVEN SKILLFULLY AVOIDS THE NUMEROUS EXPLOSIONS...
BAM
BAM
BAM

**Don't miss LEGO LEGENDS OF CHIMA #2 "The Right Decision"
available now at booksellers everywhere!**